ON THE STREET
WHERE YOU
DIE

Al Stevens

Mockingbird
Songs & Stories

Mockingbird Songs & Stories, Cocoa, FL

ISBN-13: 978-0-9886623-4-6

ON THE STREET WHERE YOU DIE

Dedication

To the memory of Frederick W. Stevens, Sr.

Acknowledgments

Thanks to Joy Seymore for her suggestions and corrections to this story.

Chapter 1

On the afternoon when all this trouble started I was sitting alone in my office, reading the newspaper, and waiting for cocktail hour. Or daylight savings time, whichever came first. A half-empty fifth of cheap bourbon beckoned from my desk drawer, and I tried with good intentions to ignore its call. But when there's no work for a private investigator and no woman in his life, drinking is what's left. Come to think of it, it's also what's left when you're busy and getting laid.

The outer door opened and closed, and footsteps sounded across the floor.

"A client?" I said to no one at all.

A client was just what the bill collector ordered. Business had slowed to a crawl. Blame it on the economy. People were staying married, in jail, at home, or some combination of the three. Times were tough.

I looked at my Mickey Mouse wristwatch. Don't laugh. It's all I got in the divorce. It was a few minutes past four, and Willa had gone home. I was about to get up and go greet the visitor when the door to my office opened. André the Giant stood in the doorway.

He hadn't knocked. Good thing I wasn't doing the bottle, scratching my nuts, or anything else private.

The light was directly behind him, and his height, broad shoulders, Al Capone fedora, and alpaca overcoat presented an imposing silhouette.

"Come in and sit down," I said to the imposing silhouette. I took off my reading glasses and put them on the desk.

In my business, a big guy coming in uninvited and unexpected could be bad news. I made a fast mental inventory of cheating husbands I might have pissed off and bail jumpers I had restored to the judicial system, and none of them had been anywhere near that big.

My gun was in the safe. Plan ahead.

The big man moved into the light. The desk lamp cast shadows upwards on his face giving him a fierce, chiseled look, hardened and set with a bigger jaw than anybody needed. His blue-gray eyes scanned the room and settled on me.

The alpaca overcoat was expensive. So were the spit-shined imported alligator-skin shoes, the cost of either one of which would have paid for my car and bought a tank of gas and a year's insurance, neither of which I had at the moment. A man of means. A big man of means.

"Mr. Bentworth?" the big man of means said.

"That's the name on the door," I said. Not exactly the snappiest of repartees, but the best I could come up with on short notice. I've done better and am known for it.

The stranger shifted from side to side and adjusted his shoulders as if to take a more at-the-ready stance.

I fidgeted in my chair, and my skivvies wedged into the crack of my ass. Why does that always happen just when you can't do anything about it? One of life's small mysteries.

"Call me Stan," I said. "And you are?"

He pulled a chair over and removed his cream-colored wool felt fedora. He dropped the hat on the desk, spun the chair around backwards, and lowered himself onto the seat, his arms on the back, his knees high on either side of him. He looked around the room again and took in the office accoutrements. It didn't take long. There wasn't much to take in. A desk, two chairs, a safe, and a coat rack.

All that and me rutching around in my swivel chair from cheek to cheek trying to get my skivvies to pop out on their own. It never works.

"Sergeant Penrod says you're the man I need," the big guy said. He was articulate with a cultured voice that belied his tough guy stature and bearing. "He says you know how to find people."

"That's my specialty. Who's lost?"

"Someone is putting the squeeze on me. I need to find out who."

"What kind of squeeze?" I said.

He looked around again. "You don't look all that prosperous."

"My needs are simple. Who's shaking you down, Mr...?"

"Overbee. Buford Overbee. You ever hear that name?"

I stifled a smile at the notion of a man who looked like Hulk Hogan having a name like Buford Overbee. But who am I to question a guy's name? How many private dicks do you meet named Stanley?

"Can't say I have," I said. "So who needs finding?" I sat back, folded my arms, and waited.

He looked around the room again. "Never heard of me, huh? Buford Overbee?" He emphasized both halves of the name and seemed disappointed that I didn't recognize it.

"Nope. So, when are you going to tell me who you need found? I got to be somewhere Tuesday."

"Don't get your briefs in a bunch," he said. "I'm getting there."

I wished he hadn't mentioned briefs. Mine were still tucked up my ass.

"Bill Penrod recommended me?"

"He did."

"He works homicide," I said. "I hope you don't want somebody killed."

"I want somebody found."

"What's his name?"

"Don't know."

"Where's he live?"

"Don't know."

"What's he look like?"

"Don't know."

"I charge more for don't know, don't know, and don't know."

"Money's no problem."

My kind of client. "Makes things easier," I said.

"If you're willing to take this job, I'll give you a few days to see what you can do."

He opened his wallet, took out a handful of hundred dollar bills, and put the stack on the desk.

"That's a thousand. Will it do for a retainer?"

I looked at the stack lovingly. This month's rent and some left over for necessities. Such as bourbon.

"It will if I take the job, which I haven't decided."

That was bullshit. I was going to take the job. Whatever it involved. If he wanted Jimmy Hoffa found, I was going to take the job.

"Keep the dough. If you don't want the job, it'll be hush money to keep your yap shut about what I'm about to tell you. Does that work?"

I picked up the thousand, swiveled around, and put it in the safe.

"I'll take that for a yes," he said.

He stood and turned the chair around the way it was meant to be. He sat, put his elbows on the desk, and rested his Jay Leno chin in his Michael Jordan hands.

"Make no mistake," he said. "I expect you to honor the confidentiality I just purchased."

"Mr. Overbee, I didn't invite you here just to get a lecture on professional ethics."

"You didn't invite me at all. I let myself in."

"Fair enough."

He got up, hung his coat on the coat rack, came back, and plopped down again. He shifted around. He was too big for that chair. His butt hung over the sides, and his knees were at chest level. He stared at me. Then after a moment he said, "What we are about to discuss is a matter of life and death."

"Whose life and whose death?" I hoped he didn't mean mine.

"If you find the guy, it could be his. If you don't, it might be mine."

"Sounds serious enough. Who is it? Inquiring minds and all that."

It didn't matter who the target was. In my current situation I would have found his cat if the fee was there.

I shook a cigarette out of the pack on my desk and offered one to Overbee. He shook his head. This would be my last cigarette. I was determined to quit smoking.

Overbee waited while I lit up, took a long drag, and exhaled a plume of blue smoke into the room. Then he said, "The guy I want found is shaking me down, and if I don't pay him, I could get killed."

"By whom?"

"There are people looking for me. He could tell them where I am."

"Who's looking for you?"

"Still not convinced you're right for this job," he said.

"Well, I'd certainly try to convince you if you'd only tell me more about the fucking job."

He looked me up and down. "You talk tougher than you look."

"If you want somebody found, I'm your man. If you're looking for muscle, I'm not it."

"I can tell."

I wish people wouldn't be so quick to notice that.

He continued. "Suppose when I came in here, I came to beat the shit out of you. What would happen?"

I looked him up and down. "You'd beat the shit out of me." I paused. "Assuming you could catch me."

"You don't think I'd catch you?"

"You'd be slipping in shit the whole way."

Not even a smile. Jokes were wasted on Overbee.

"What about the street?" he said. "How do you handle trouble?"

"Mr. Overbee—"

"Buford," Overbee said.

"Buford. The wise and noble framers of our great Constitution bestowed upon us the right to own and bear arms."

That's an argument never lost on a real man. Or so they tell me.

"How are you with computers?" he asked. "I don't see one here." He looked around the room again. I wished he'd quit looking around the room.

"I get by with them, but I have a guy who's a whiz."

"How good is he?"

"Well, I'm not saying Bill Gates calls him whenever he can't figure something out, but he could. Now tell me more."

He took a deep breath and said, "I'll start with a warning." That caught my attention, and I leaned forward. "There are those," he said, "who would do anything to know what you are about to learn. My life wouldn't be worth a dime if they found it out. Anyone who knows who and where I am could be in similar danger if the wrong people find out. Do you want me to proceed?"

I sat for a moment and cogitated about what he could say that would put me in danger just for knowing it. Who was Buford Overbee? Who wanted to know? I was hooked and wasn't going to pass up hearing this story.

"Proceed," I said.

"I used to have other interests that, if exposed, could compromise the fiduciary trust that I enjoy with my clients."

"Clients?"

"Investors. I have a dubious past, you might say."

"How dubious?"

"I used to work for the mob."

I dropped my pencil on the desk and sat back in my chair with a thump.

"Are these the guys I should be afraid of?" I said.

"Everybody should be afraid of them."

I couldn't sense any fear coming from him, but what do I know? I'm a wimp. He's Jesse Ventura.

"What was your job back then?"

"Collections."

Which meant if you owed the mob money, Buford would encourage you to do the right thing and meet your obligations. He looked qualified for that line of work.

"Got it. Did you use words like 'fiduciary trust' when you were a wise guy?"

"No."

"So now something's backfired."

"It has. I'm being blackmailed."

"Well, I'm shocked." I leaned back in my chair and raised my eyebrows. "Given all the mobsters and shady investors you've done business with, it saddens me that someone would sink that low. What's this world coming to?"

He didn't crack a smile.

"Who do you think is putting the clamp on your nuts?" I asked.

He shrugged and raised his hands palms up. "That's the problem, Stan. I don't have a clue. He's anonymous."

This wasn't going to be easy. I looked at my watch, the Timex with Mickey Mouse on the dial.

"It's almost six. You want a drink?"

Overbee looked at his watch, a Rolex with diamonds on the dial. "It isn't almost six, and yeah, I want a drink."

I opened a desk drawer and took out the bottle and two glasses. I poured myself a drink, started to pour one for Overbee, and stopped.

"If you're worried about the glass being dirty, and it probably is, there's running water down the hall."

"Pour."

Nothing could live in that kerosene anyway. I poured and we each took a healthy swig. The bourbon burned going down. I took another gulp to put out the fire. It didn't work.

After his first swig, he scrunched up his nose and mouth.

"You don't like bourbon?" I asked.

"I do. And next time I'll bring some." He sniffed his glass, closed his eyes, and shook his head.

"Let's don't drink this horse piss," I said. "We can go across the street. They pour a good drink at Oliver's."

He stood up and got his alpaca overcoat from the rack. I stood up, and my skivvies popped out of the crack of my ass. At last.

Chapter 2

Delbert Falls is a typical medium-sized town in Maryland, between Baltimore and Philadelphia. My office is in the northwest section, which has low-rent industrial and commercial buildings and a few low-rent apartment buildings.

"Elevator out of order?" Buford said.

"I don't think there is an elevator. The doors and buttons are just for show."

We went down the stairs and across the street to Oliver's, a small saloon that serves an ample drink at a reasonable price.

We took a booth for the privacy. Sammy came over with my usual, a double Jack neat.

"This is Sammy," I said, "my closest friend and confidant."

Buford reached up to shake hands. "I'm Buford. I'll have the same."

Sammy went to the bar to get Buford's drink.

"You can trust Sammy," I said. "The soul of discretion."

"Every good bartender is," Buford said.

Sammy brought Buford's drink and returned to the bar. Buford looked at his glass for a while then took a sip.

"This is better." He took a cigar from his pocket and lit it. I lit my last cigarette ever. I was going to quit. Did I already say that?

"Penrod said you used to be a cop."

"I was. We were partners. Homicide."

"Tell me why you're doing this and not a cop anymore. It can't be for the money."

I didn't like telling this story. But everyone wants to hear it. I should just go on Jerry Springer.

9

"Got canned," I said. "I was a good cop. Caught killers. Closed cases."

"And they let you go?"

"That's a nice way of putting it. I took a swing at a suspect. He swung back. End of fight. With me as first runner-up. According to the bosses, they can't have suspects beating the shit out of detectives in the squad room. Makes them look bad."

"They fired you for losing a fight?"

"They did. If only that citizen hadn't been there with his cell phone. Click. Smile. You're on candid Youtube. And the six o'clock news."

"I can see where that would piss off the brass."

He shifted around. His girth took up most of the bench.

"Punching that moke was the last straw, according to the Lieutenant. Came as a surprise. I didn't know I had been piling up straws."

"Sauce?"

My secret was out.

"Yeah. The Lieutenant was one of those guys who bores the shit out of you with his endless litany about the evils of drink, meetings, twelve steps, one day at a time, and all that shit."

"I know the type. I married his sister." He took another drink.

"He asked who my enabler was."

"Your what?"

"Someone who encourages the drinking. Like my ex-wife. And maybe your wife. They nag you about your drinking so you drink more to block it out."

I looked towards the bar and said, "I told him these days my enabler is Sammy."

We both took slow sips. Buford took another pull on his cigar. I lit another last cigarette.

"So you wound up a P.I."

"After I retired without a pension, I got a license, had cards printed, and painted my name on the door. It was that or be a Walmart greeter."

"You like this line of work?"

"If I have to work for assholes, I might as well be self-employed."

"And now you find missing persons."

"Runaway teenagers, deadbeat dads, bail jumpers, cheating spouses, hidden assets. The usual."

I downed the last of my bourbon.

"Now," I said, "are you going to give me some details about the shakedown or are you going to have another drink?"

"Yes," he said.

I signaled to Sammy to bring another round. I took a pencil and pad from my trench coat pocket. I don't always take notes, but detectives on TV do it, and it's expected.

Like most clients, Buford recited his life story first, something I usually don't care about, but if you don't let them spill their guts, they'll keep trying. So, I am a good listener. A booth in a bar can be a kind of confessional.

"I'm a financier. Investment counselor. Big money. High-profile clientele. Moguls, movie stars, politicians. You ever read the financial section of the newspaper? Or the Wall Street Journal?"

"No. I figured I'd take that up after I make my second million."

"Already made your first?" He was probably wondering if I was a potential client.

"No. Gave up on that. Working on my second."

"That's why you don't know my name. I make a lot of money in investments."

"Ponzi? Like Madoff?"

"No. Not yet anyway. I know my shit. My clients all made money in 2008. There's a Rolls parked in the alley behind your office with a driver waiting to take me home to a twenty-two year old wife in a big house in the Heights. I want to keep the Rolls, the driver, and the house. Not to mention the wife. I need to hang onto my money."

"And you need help with that?"

"I do."

"To help you find a blackmailer."

Buford leaned back and crossed his arms. His cigar hung out over his suit jacket, and the ash grew longer with each puff. I waited for it to drop off and burn a hole in the expensive garment.

"I wasn't always a successful investment counselor," he said.

"Were you an unsuccessful investment counselor?"

"No. I mean, I got into investments late in life. I'm good at it."

"You don't look like the typical investment counselor."

"What do I look like?" he asked.

"More like the typical biker bar bouncer. Except for the clothes. You got tattoos under those threads?"

He ignored my sarcasm and took a long drag on his cigar. The ash grew longer.

"I know you're a big mother," I said, "but how does a guy with a moniker like Buford Overbee get a job as a wise guy?"

Buford smiled for the first time. "That wasn't my name back then. I changed it when I went into this line of work. More respectable, more impressive."

"More anonymous."

"Right. I chose a name that doesn't look like me. Not only do my present clients not know about my past, my former employers don't know about my present. I keep a low profile. No pictures, no interviews. The press refers to me as 'the elusive Buford Overbee.' Like Howard Hughes in his later years. Always in the action but never in the picture."

The cigar ash was due to fall off on its own. He flicked it off in the ash tray. Now I could breathe again.

"What was your name before?" I asked.

"You don't need that."

"Why not?"

"Because your knowing that could draw the attention of the boys back home."

"And they'd come after me to learn what I know?"

"They would."

"How would they know that I know?" This was getting complicated.

"Stan, you're going to come into contact with some of my people and, I hope, the blackmailer himself. These kinds of secrets are hard to keep."

"You don't trust your people?"

"I don't trust anyone. Remember, the family pays well for information. Like if you tell them what they want to know, you get to keep your arms and legs."

He still had some secrets, even from me, his personal detective as of a thousand bucks ago. I'd have to break down that wall eventually, but not yet.

"I assume there's a reason you don't want your previous colleagues in the family to know where you are."

"A very big reason having to do with a grand jury and a federal prosecutor."

"Okay," I said. "I'm guessing that after testifying, you joined the witness protection country club."

"I did."

"And that's how they don't know where you are."

"It is."

"And the blackmailer, whoever it is, figured it all out."

"Apparently."

I reached my arms out and stretched them behind me on the back of the bench.

"How does a wise guy from the streets choose investment counselor as a cover profession? Why not something easy like brain surgeon or theoretical physicist?"

"I always had a feel for the market. I learned the ins and outs of insider trading when I was connected. You can do great things if you don't have scruples and don't have to worry about being caught."

"Which you don't when the feds are your guardian angels," I said.

"Which they are as long as you can be helpful."

"How do you build up a list of clients when you're an unknown, new investment counselor recently retired from the mob? Cold calls? Door-to-door?"

Imagine a guy his size knocking on your door selling mutual funds.

"I scammed my way into it."

Why did that not surprise me?

He continued. "I sent e-mails to about two hundred investors and told half of them that a particular stock would go up and the other half it would drop. Whichever way it went, I removed the other half from my list and did it again with another stock."

"I can see where this is going," I said.

"I did it three times. After that, I had a list of twenty-five investors that had just gotten three consecutive hot tips. I sent them invitations to be clients. Most of them signed on. After that it was word of mouth."

"After that you had to deliver."

"And I do."

"And now somebody has found you and wants to be paid for his silence."

"Exactly. He uses e-mail and requires online payments, for chrissake, using OnlinePay."

"What's that?"

"You send money using the Internet."

Learn something new every day.

"How much dust does he want?"

"Started out twenty grand, which I paid. But it seems that's only the first installment. Apparently this goes on forever. This time he wants thirty. I can't do that. Twenty grand here, thirty grand there, it adds up."

I couldn't argue with that.

"I want it stopped," he said. "Not just because of the money, but because I don't want some scumbag knowing he got one over on me. I hate that. That's where you come in, Stan. Find out who and where he is. You say that's your specialty? That's what I'm buying. You find him. I'll take it from there."

"I just have to find someone whose name, address, and likeness we don't know. Should be easy enough."

That was a bluff.

"All I have is his e-mail address. Can you do anything with that?"

"Well, that will take some serious hacking. I'll call in Rodney."

Rodney was my nephew, my sister's boy.

"Rodney?"

"My computer expert. When he's not working for me, he surfs for porn and breaks into government computers. Just for the hell of it."

"You sure a guy like that is reliable? Sounds flaky."

"I'm sure. When it comes to computers, if he can't do it, it can't be done."

"Okay. What's your fee?"

"Five hundred a day plus expenses."

I seldom got that much, but if you don't ask...

"What kind of expenses?"

"Travel, bribes, tips for information, whatever I have to pay Rodney, and such."

"Makes sense."

"For now I need the e-mail address of the blackmailer. And a way to reach you."

Buford took a card from his wallet and wrote on the back. "This is his e-mail address. My cell and e-mail are on the other side. Don't pass them around."

I looked at the card. "I'll need your home address."

"No, you won't. You need to talk to me, call. You can e-mail or text an invoice when you need to be paid. Just don't try to outbid the blackmailer. Keep me in the loop too. Daily progress reports."

"Will do."

"Stan, you do this for me and your financial worries are eased a bit. I'll keep you on retainer for as long as I might have these kinds of problems."

That was the best news I'd heard all day. "Don't worry, Buford. I'll find the rat."

We shook hands and Buford threw a twenty on the table and left. I went to the front window and watched him cross the street and go behind my building to the alley. Soon a white Rolls Royce Phantom pulled out of the side street and turned north. I couldn't see the driver. But the big man in the alpaca coat and fedora was in the back seat lighting another cigar. The Rolls sped away.

I ordered another drink.

Chapter 3

I must have spent the night in my car. That's where I woke up. My head pounded like the bass drum in a street band. Thump, thump. My stomach churned like a cement mixer.

I got out of the car, went into my office building, and climbed the stairs to the third floor. There seemed to be more stairs today than usual.

I've got to talk to the landlord about that elevator. It hasn't worked since before Nixon resigned. But then he'll talk to me about the rent. Which hasn't been paid since...well, you get the idea.

I went in the door marked, "Bentworth Detective Agency, LLC." I had lettered that sign myself. It showed. The door opened into Willa's office, which served as a waiting room and reception lobby. My office was behind hers with a closed door that separated us. The two offices could have used some paint, and the few pieces of furniture were more suited for the land fill, but clients didn't seem to mind. Like Buford, they had problems to be solved, and most of them cared more about results than about how my office looked.

Willa was already there, settled at her desk, looking in a hand mirror, and adjusting her makeup, a wasted effort. She was in her fifties with graying hair, square-rimmed reading glasses, and was as skinny as a fourteen-ounce pool cue. Today she was wearing a drab one-piece suit and Eleanor Roosevelt shoes.

Willa had come to work the previous year and was the most efficient office manager I'd ever had. For the first time in my long and illustrious career as a P.I., my files were in order, my schedule organized, my books balanced, and my bank account reconciled. Overdrawn but reconciled.

17

Rodney was waiting for me in my office, sitting in my chair reading a comic book with his feet up on my desk. I stood in the doorway, bleary-eyed and head throbbing, and looked at him.

"What's up Uncle Stanley?" Rodney was too cheerful for this kind of morning. Hell, Ebenezer Scrooge before the ghosts would have been too cheerful. My mouth felt like I'd been licking the bottom of a bird cage, the ringing in my ears would have rivaled the Anvil Chorus, and my asshole felt like Johnny Cash's burning ring of fire. I didn't dare fart. They'd have had to pick me up somewhere near Cleveland.

If you need any more hangover metaphors, come back tomorrow.

I made my usual morning-after resolution to quit drinking. This time I meant it. Like all the other times.

Rodney made no move to vacate my desk. He was tall and gangly with spiked orange hair. He was dressed in the usual baggy shorts, the top of which was down around the lower part of his ass with the crotch at his knees.

"Rodney, what holds those pants up?"

He put the comic book on the table and turned the swivel chair to face me.

"Will power," he said.

"Get up," I said.

He stood up and walked past me. I sat down.

"Your Jockey shorts are showing," I said.

"That's the style." He turned to face me.

"I hope you change them every day."

"Yellow in front, brown in back."

His T-shirt said, "If God hadn't meant for man to eat pussy, He wouldn't have made it look like a taco." The back of the shirt had a picture of a vertical taco.

"Damn, Rodney. That shirt can get you arrested. Does your mother know about it?"

"She bought it."

My sister. What a piece of work.

"Why are you here?" I asked.

"You called last night. Said we have a job."

"I did? Oh, yeah, I did." I didn't remember the call, but we did have work. "Got your laptop?"

"Yeah, in my backpack."

"If I give you an e-mail address, can you find out whose it is and where they are?"

His backpack hung from a hook on the coat rack. He got it, pulled the other chair over, unpacked the laptop, and set it up on the desk.

"Usually," he said. "It can take some time depending on whether it's through a website service or a dedicated mail server. One way or other I have to hack into the server with its IP address, crack the password file, get root privileges—"

"I don't need details, Rodney." If I'd let him, he'd give me the history of hacking all the way back to Babbage.

I wrote the blackmailer's e-mail address on a slip of paper and gave it to him. "How long will it take?"

"Better part of the day," he said.

That meant about an hour. Rodney always overestimated.

"I might not find out where the guy is located," he said. "He can log on from anywhere. But I can probably get his name and sometimes his home address."

"That'll be enough. When you're done with that, I'll have another job for you. Use my desk. I'll be gone for a while. Breakfast."

Just saying the word turned my stomach. But often food was the only way out of a hangover.

"Can I smoke in here?"

"Smoke what?"

"Shit."

"No."

"You drink in here."

"Booze is legal, Rodney, and won't cost me my P.I. ticket, and it doesn't get into the draperies."

"What draperies?"

"I keep meaning to get draperies. Anyway, keep the shit in your backpack."

I got the thousand bucks out of the safe, left Rodney to his hacking, and went into the outer office.

"Most secretaries would have brought coffee to the boss by now," I said to Willa.

"Most secretaries get paid with some degree of regularity."

I handed her Buford's stack of hundred-dollar bills.

"What's this?" she asked.

"What's it look like?"

"I don't know," she said, counting the money. "It's been so long."

Everybody's a smartass today.

I shrugged. "Pay some bills with it."

"Can I start with my back pay?"

"If you must."

"I must."

"Will it cover what I owe you?"

"No. But I won't take it all."

I sat on the edge of her desk. "Start a file, Willa. New client. Name of Buford Overbee."

"You're kidding," she said. She was making notes.

"You've heard of him?"

"Who hasn't?"

"Me. Wait'll you see him."

"Nobody's ever seen him. Address?"

"Don't have one. Here's his phone number and e-mail." I gave her the card.

She wrote down the contact information and turned the card over. "Whose e-mail is this on the back?"

"It's relevant to the case."

"Relevant e-mail address," she said and made more notes. She gave the card back to me.

"Don't send any e-mail to that address. Its owner doesn't know we have it. Doesn't even know about us."

"Whatever. I suppose you'll explain later."

"If I have to. I'm out of here. Got to get some breakfast. Hope I can hold it down."

"Get some breath mints too, Stan. Whatever you were celebrating last night is still with us. You've got a breath on you would wither crab grass across the Interstate."

Only a true friend would tell you that.

She opened a drawer and began rummaging in it. "Now where did I put that Lysol spray?"

"Don't worry. It won't get into the draperies."

"What dr—? Oh, get the hell out of here."

I went across the street to Ray's diner, my usual eating place. It was in a brick building, now mostly unoccupied. Ray grilled the best burger on either side of the tracks, and his loyal clientele kept him in business.

Bunny was on duty. I was always glad to see Bunny. She had been my on-again, off-again girlfriend for about seven years. Even when we were off-again, like now, we stayed friends. Not many women in my life had been able to do that. My breakups had always been noisy and unpleasant. Not with Bunny, though. We'd just agree that time had come to move on, usually at her initiative. Then after some time off, we'd try again. This was one of those times when we weren't trying.

One of those off-again periods had given me a low time in my life. I tried marriage. A failed experiment. I was not cut out for wedlock. Neither was my wife. It came to an end when she ran off with my best friend. I sure do miss him.

When the divorce was final, I got back with Bunny, which lasted less than a year, ending when she met the man of her dreams, which was how it usually ended. That was six months ago. As usual, we remained friends, a necessity because of Ray's cooking.

I figured Bunny would go easy on a guy in a divorce, a hell of a criterion for choosing a girlfriend, but with experience comes wisdom. And caution.

Bunny had been the perfect girlfriend. She didn't spend our times together saying what an asshole her ex-husband was. Or what she'd do when she won the lottery. Or snore.

I took a seat in a booth and looked out the window at the run-down building that housed my office across the street. The building hadn't aged well.

Then I looked at Bunny. She had aged well. She still looked good for an old broad. Sexy women who take care of themselves stay sexy as time passes. Bunny had taken care of herself. A little wider in the middle and at the hips and a few lines on her face, but it was only a matter of perspective. I'd been without female companionship since we broke up. A couple more months of that and Grandma Walton would have looked good.

She leaned against the booth and crossed one ankle over the other. Her skirt was just above the knees. Her knees had aged well.

"Hi, Stan. You look like shit."

"Good to see you too."

"Maybe if you'd shave. Or change your shirt."

"Or blow my brains out."

"What happened? The usual?"

"Yep. Hangover. Chronic."

She poured me a cup of coffee and scribbled on her order pad without asking what I wanted. Bunny knew I'd eat whatever she brought. Like being married but without the baggage. Ham or bacon and eggs, usually. Eggs cooked however it fancied her. Eggs didn't sound so good this morning. I figured I might be able to get down a feather soufflé if I took it slow.

Bunny put the order through the window to Ray in the kitchen, came back, sat across from me, and handed me a mint. Subtle, but effective.

"So, what's new?" she asked.

"Same ol', same ol'," I said.

"What were you celebrating?"

"Got a new client."

"So, did you have to drink up the whole fee in one night."

"He helped. I don't drink alone. Unless there's nobody around."

"Another husband with a cheating wife?"

"No, a financier." I lowered my voice. I could trust Bunny. Well, to a point. "Guy named Overbee."

"I've heard of him," she said. "He's been in some kind of deep shit for hustling hedge funds."

Was I the only person who never heard of my client?

"What's a hedge fund?" I asked.

"Beats me," she said. "But apparently they can get you in deep shit. The TV news people are all over each other trying to get him on camera. Nobody knows what he looks like."

"I do."

"So? What's he look like?"

"Big guy. Good looking in a rough kind of way. You'd like him. Reminds me of that jerk you dumped me for last time. B-B-B-Barry, the body builder. He still around?"

"No. It didn't last. Barry was too much into himself. Muscle shirts and never met a mirror he didn't love. If we weren't talking about Barry, he'd change the subject. And I couldn't stand the stutter."

She wiped the table with her cloth. It didn't need it, but it gave her something to look busy with while we talked.

"So Overbee looks like Barry?" she said.

She sounded interested. "Some. But older. Don't get your hopes up. He has a twenty-two year old wife."

"Don't they all?"

I looked at her some more. The hangover got in the way, but I still found her attractive. I always felt like she found me convenient rather than attractive.

"So you're available again?" I said.

"Who said I'm available?"

"Just guessing. B-B-B-Barry's out of the picture, and your body language has an allure to it, that unmistakable seductive, sensuous come-hither quality. That's usually a good sign."

"I don't know what that means."

"Neither do I, but it worked the last time I used it."

She laughed, got up, refilled my coffee, and went to see about my breakfast.

While I waited, Rodney came in and sat down.

"I thought you'd be here," he said. "Here's the name and address you wanted."

He handed me a sheet of paper with the name Mario Vitole scrawled on it along with a phone number and an address in a residential section on the south side of town.

"Vitole. Sounds like a wise guy. Good work, Rodney. Didn't take that long."

"Yeah, it was easy. The guy's mail server is local. Here in town. It runs under an old version of Linux. I got in by downloading the password file and decrypting—"

"That's okay. You want breakfast?"

"No, I had a Hershey Bar and a Coke."

"Don't talk like that when I'm hung over. Here's your next assignment."

I took out Buford's card, took a napkin from the dispenser, and copied down Buford's cell phone number.

"Can you find out where the owner of this cell phone lives based on the number? It's our client's cell."

"You don't know where your client lives?"

"No. He keeps a lot to himself. Can you get his address?"

Rodney shrugged and put the napkin in his pocket. "I can do better than that. If he's got the GPS turned on, I can find out where he is at any time."

"That works. Wherever he spends his nights is probably his house. It'll be in the Heights. But how can you do that? Without too much geek-speak, please. Can anyone do it?"

I was thinking about my own cell phone and whether I could be tracked too.

"No. You need software. The FBI has it on their main server."

"And of course you can get into the FBI's server." Nothing about Rodney's computer skills surprised me any more.

"Easy. I've done it a bunch of times. You start by—"

"Can I turn off the GPS in my own phone?"

"Yes. In the Settings app."

He took my phone and showed me how to disable the GPS.

"And that prevents the FBI and geeks like you from tracking me?"

"Sure does."

"Good to know. Okay, try to get this guy's home address. Get back to me when you got it."

Rodney got up to leave. I said, "Sit down. There's one more thing."

He sat.

"Our client is being blackmailed. The owner of that e-mail address you hacked is the blackmailer. He uses an OnlinePay account for the payoffs. You know what that is?"

"Yep."

"Can you hack into that account?"

"Yep. I just need to—"

"What can you do once you've hacked in there?"

"I can do anything he can do. Get the balance, send money to someone, transfer money to another account, and like that. You see, the service's main server—"

"Don't do it yet. But we might need to later. I'll be back in the office after breakfast."

Speaking of breakfast, Bunny brought it. She sat it down in front of me, looked at Rodney, and read the inscription on his taco shirt. She almost choked and snorted to keep from laughing, turned, and hurried back into the kitchen.

After Rodney left, I looked carefully at my breakfast. The sight and smell of bacon and eggs probably would have made me hurl right there in the diner, but Bunny had been gentle. Oatmeal, cantaloupe, and a slice of unbuttered wheat toast.

Why do we call it "unbuttered?" It makes it sound like the toast was previously buttered and someone removed the butter. It should be "non-buttered." Same with "unsweetened." I worry about shit like that.

Bunny came out of the kitchen and sat down across from me. "Enjoy. You want to talk?"

"You talk," I said, my mouth full of non-buttered toast. "I'll chew."

She pushed forward so that her tits rested on the tabletop. I kind of choked on a swallow of oatmeal. She knew what she was doing.

"About me being available. I guess I am. You interested?"

Here we go again. I swallowed the oatmeal, washed it down with coffee, wiped my mouth with a napkin, and looked her in the face, not easy to do when her boobs were rubbing back and forth on the table and showing their cleavage inside her non-buttoned blouse. She had that doe-eyed look that always made me wilt. She knew it too.

"You know, Bunny, we've been down this road before."

"Yeah, and maybe we'll go down it again. And maybe not." She pulled away from the table, looked around the diner and ran her hand through her hair. "I'm getting a little long in the tooth, Stan. I'm not the hottie I used to be. You got a better chance of hanging on to me now."

Bunny had given me a picture of herself in a two-piece bathing suit. I kept it in my desk drawer. With the onset of middle age, she had gone down a few notches on the Bo Derrick scale and had to lower her standards and go out with guys like me. Until she found better, that is. Then it would turn into the old maybe-we-should-see-other-people, let's-stay-friends routine. What could you do?

I shook my head. "It sure flatters a guy when a woman wants him only because she's too old to attract younger men."

"I thought you'd feel that way. I'm sorry. You want to go out for a drink tonight?"

"I quit drinking?"

"Bullshit. When?"

"About a half hour ago when I realized that a fried egg would decorate the linoleum. So I'm off the sauce. It's easier to give up than eating."

"We've been down that road too."

"Yes, we have."

"Well, think about it. Stop by at quitting time if you're willing. Since you're on the wagon, maybe you can come by my place for a taco."

She laughed again and returned to the kitchen.

Chapter 4

I finished my breakfast, left money on the table, and headed back across the street to the office. I felt better already. Must have been the healthy breakfast.

The day looked like a nice one for late autumn. It was chilly, and I pulled my trench coat around me, but the sun was shining, and the wind was down. I went in the building and climbed the stairs, an easier climb than this morning's. I went in and took off my trench coat.

"Any messages, Willa?"

"Your sister called. Not urgent."

"Anything left from that thousand?"

"No."

"We still in debt?"

"Yes."

I sounded out Willa on the Bunny situation.

"I got news. Bunny's back on the market," I said.

"So?"

"She wants me back."

Willa sniffed. "That's not news. For how long this time?"

I couldn't answer that.

"You know how this is going to turn out," she said. "Just like always."

I didn't want that debate so I changed the subject. "You think I'd be more attractive to women if I took up body building?"

"Maybe if you built one from scratch. Not much to work with there." She laughed.

"Thanks a lot. I just don't know how to hang onto a woman. Particularly one who goes for younger men."

"Rogaine, a face lift, liposuction, and AA might help. Not in that order."

Willa didn't approve of my drinking. I didn't want to get into that one either, so I went into my office.

Rodney was at my desk, his face in the laptop, his fingers tapping the keys faster than the notes in a Kenny G solo.

I sat in the guest chair, took out my phone, and called my sister.

"Hi, Mandy, what's up?"

"Is Rodney there?" she asked.

"Yes. He's here working on a problem for me."

"He ought to be in school."

"He graduated, remember?"

"I mean in college. Smart kid like that. Can he hear us?"

"No. Did you buy him that shirt?"

"What shirt?"

"The one with the taco on it."

She giggled. "I bought that for me to wear to aerobics. He keeps taking it."

"Burn it. What do you need, Mandy?"

"I've been seeing a guy, an Army Captain assigned to where I work. We've been out a few times to the Officer's Club and out on his boat. A real nice river cruiser. He's got my phone number, but when I ask for his, he changes the subject."

"What's his name? Where's he live?"

"Jeremy Pugh. Somewhere around here. I don't know exactly where."

"I'll call you back," I said and clicked off the phone.

I couldn't blame the guy for liking Amanda. She was in her early thirties, a pretty, single mom with only Rodney to worry about. She got all the beauty genes in our family. She did not, however, get the brainy genes, and she counted on me to solve most of life's problems.

"Rodney," I said.

He stopped typing and looked up.

"Look up Captain Jeremy Pugh somewhere in the Metro area, and get me his home number."

"Is that the prick Mom's been going out with?"

"That's the prick."

After some rapid-fire keystrokes, Rodney read off a phone number.

I keyed the number on my phone and waited. A woman's voice answered.

"Mrs. Pugh?"

"Yes?" She was a young woman. Not the Captain's mother, I'd bet.

"Is Captain Pugh there?"

"Why no. He's at work."

"Okay. I must have missed him. Is this the Captain's wife?"

"Yes, this is Bernadine Pugh."

"Okay, ma'am. Sorry to have troubled you."

I rang off and called Amanda again.

"He's married, Mandy."

Silence. Then, "I was afraid of that. My usual luck. What do I do now? I'm supposed to go out with him again on Friday. Meeting him at the O club."

"Stand him up. His wife's name is Bernadine. If he troubles you again, tell him you'll call her. Or his Commanding Officer. Or me."

"How'd you find out?"

"Good, solid police work. Comes from years of experience. I looked him up in the phone book and called. His wife answered."

"Thanks, Stanley."

I rang off and put the phone on the desk. Rodney looked up.

"What was all that about," he asked.

"Your Mom. Made another bad choice."

"The Captain?"

"That's the one. What's he like?"

"Average guy. You know."

"Seem to be the combat type? Like maybe a Ranger? Afghanistan or something?"

"Him? No. What's Mom going to do?"

"Don't know."

"She'll never learn," Rodney said.

"She never will," I said.

He pointed to the laptop. "Okay, Uncle Stanley. Look at this."

I rolled the chair around to see the screen. It displayed a page with the FBI logo and a street map, crosshairs on the map, and some text in an adjacent box.

"This is where the client's cell phone is right now," Rodney said, indicating the crosshairs. "It's in the Heights just like you said."

"I wonder if that's his residence or an office."

"Wait."

Rodney clicked and typed. A big picture of the earth displayed. It spun and zoomed in and stopped with an overhead view of a street and some houses. More clicks and the monitor showed the front of the house, a large mansion with a circular, tree-lined driveway.

"Nice place," I said. "I'll have to pay a visit to my old drinking buddy Buford."

"Can I go?" Rodney asked.

"Not dressed like that, you can't. That's a gated community. One look at that shirt and hairdo, and the security guard slams the gate down and calls the cops."

"You don't look all that spiffy yourself, Uncle Stanley."

"Yeah, well, I'm going home soon. A nap, shower and shave, and a change of clothes will get me past the guard. I think it would take more of a major overhaul for you. No offense."

"None taken. I like how I dress."

"I don't mind it all that much, but if you want to get on the client side of this business, you have to conform."

"Some day."

I pointed at the laptop. "See if you can get into the U.S. Marshals Service witness protection database."

"Let's see."

More clicking and typing.

"There," he said. "What do you need?"

"Buford Overbee. That would be the witness's new identity."

Click, click, tap, tap. "This the guy? I found him in the archives."

The screen showed front and side mug shots of Buford from about ten years ago accompanied by his description, rap sheet, and notes about his case. The physical description was about right. His hair in the photos was darker with touches of gray, and his name had been Anthony Curro. His street name was "Collector."

His rap sheet had countless minor offenses: extortion, assault, witness tampering, and the like. No convictions, though. The last charge was the big one. Murder. One dead drug dealer to account for. He had made a deal to roll on his bosses for the feds, and they lowered the charges.

The notes said that they had had an open-and-shut case with possible death penalty implications. But because the victim had been a drug dealer, they pled it down to a charge that drew time served and put Buford in witness protection.

A final notation said that Anthony Curro aka Buford Overbee aka "Collector" was no longer an active case. He had opted out of witness protection about five years ago.

Chapter 5

The northeast quadrant of Delbert Falls was the fashionable part of town. Upscale residents, large houses, even some mansions in the Heights; the town center with the county courthouse, the city police department, and city government buildings; expensive restaurants and hotels; and fashionable shopping malls catering to the more affluent citizenry. I had worked at police headquarters there when I was on the force. The Heights were uptown.

I drove north to the Interstate then a few miles east across the railroad tracks and took the exit for the Heights. A few miles to the north and I was in the Heights. A few more miles and I turned in and stopped at the guarded gate that protected residents of the Tall Oaks subdivision from invasion of the riff-raff.

The gatekeeper was an elderly fellow in a clean, pressed uniform that didn't fit. The stitched-on name tag said, "Bob." I wondered whether he was Bob or just wearing Bob's uniform.

He came out of his guard shack and went behind my car with a clipboard. He looked at my license plate and then at the clipboard.

He came to the driver's side of the car and asked, "May I help you?"

Why do people always ask that when what they really mean is, "Who the hell are you, and what the fuck are you doing here?"

So I said, "Yes you may. Open the gate."

Apparently Bob had expected a different answer. He glared at me and looked at my car, a nine year old compact station wagon with faded paint and, if you looked inside, worn upholstery and trash on the seats and floorboards. And if you didn't look inside too. Bob looked inside.

"What is your business here, sir?"

"Just that, Bob. My business."

"Who do you wish to see? I'll call and ask whether you are allowed into the compound."

The compound? What's that? Bob's request placed me in a quandary. Buford liked to keep a low profile, and I wondered whether his name was known at Bob's guard shack.

"Tell you what. I'll call him myself," I said.

Bob looked puzzled as if that had never happened. He was supposed to do the calling. I punched Buford's number into my cell phone.

"Buford, it's Stan."

"You got progress to report?"

"Yes I do. I'm sitting here at the guard shack at your compound, and Barney Fife won't let me in without authorization."

"How did you learn where I live?"

"Rodney," I said. "What about this rent-a-cop? I'd like to get in before it's time for his nap."

"Let me talk to him."

I handed the phone to Bob. After a brief conversation, he gave my phone back to me, went into the shack, and did something after which the gate raised. It made him grumpy, and he didn't wave. Denying access is control. Being ordered to allow access is subservience. Not the way to treat an armed minion of security.

I said into the phone, "Thanks, that did it."

"You'll need the address," Buford said.

"Already got it. See you in about two minutes."

I hung up before Buford could respond. I thought about peeling rubber just to piss off Bob even more, but the old heap wasn't up to it and would probably have blown a tire and dropped the transmission in the roadway.

I drove in and to the left around a circular lane with well-manicured lawns and mansions set back from the outer side of the road and a park and country club in the center. When I got to Buford's place I turned into his entranceway. Another gate and another guard shack. No one was in this one, and the gate swung open. I drove in around the circular driveway and parked at the front door.

Buford's shack was impressive. A three story colonial with a full-length front portico and Corinthian columns the height of the house. Tall windows on either side of a huge double door, which swung open when I got out of my car. Buford came out to greet me. We shook hands and went inside.

What a place. The foyer opened onto a long wide hallway and a huge circular staircase. Paneling, paintings, and stained glass lined the walls. Statues in the hallways, chandeliers, and antique furniture along the walls completed the palatial picture. It looked like the lobby of a Victorian museum. We walked past the staircase and down the halls. A row of mahogany chairs lined one side of the wall.

"Anybody ever sit in them," I asked.

"Not that I know of," Buford said. "How did you find this place?"

"Let's get settled somewhere, and I'll explain. Maybe in the ballroom, the amphitheatre, or the rugby stadium."

He pointed to a door that went out the back to an enclosed patio. "Go out there and find a seat. I'll be out soon. Ramon will bring you a drink."

He turned away, went into what looked like either a study or the British Museum library and pulled the paneled pocket doors closed.

I went into the patio area. Whenever a fictional detective goes into a mansion, there's always a beautiful young woman wearing almost no clothes, lounging around, looking bored, and ready to jump the bones of the first man who comes along. Just like real life.

I was right. A woman was there. A young woman. But not scantily clothed and not beautiful. She wore a robe and those ugly fuzzy pink slippers that women like and that look like troll feet. She was sitting in a chaise lounge reading a tabloid magazine.

Her hair was up in curlers, and she was smoking a cigarette. She looked up when I came in and returned to her magazine.

The glass-enclosed patio overlooked a large lake with clusters of trees all around it. It was late fall, and the trees were mostly bare except for the pine and fir trees. A golf course was off to one side and tennis courts to the other. The good life.

A young Latino man in a white uniform appeared out of nowhere.

"Would you like a drink, señor?"

I looked at my watch. Mickey Mouse said eleven o'clock plus or minus a few minutes. I couldn't be more precise than that. Mickey's gloved finger was too chubby.

My resolve to quit drinking was weakening so I modified it. I said to myself, "I hereby resolve to not drink too much." Then to the servant, "Bourbon, please. Neat." I was sure Buford's kerosene would be better than mine, and I looked forward to it. If I could hold it down.

"Are you Ramon?" I asked the servant.

"Si, señor." Then he turned to the young woman and said, "Does Missy care for a drink?"

The young woman nodded, and Ramon disappeared into the house.

The woman lowered her magazine and looked at me.

"It's a bit early," she said as if to explain that she didn't usually imbibe at this hour, an explanation I didn't believe.

"Not in Madagascar," I answered.

"Where's that?"

"Beats me. Are you Mrs. Overbee?" Buford had said he had a twenty-two year old wife. I expected something a little nicer than what was sprawled out lounging a few feet away, however. Her age was right, but this tomato had not taken care of herself.

"No, I'm Miss Curro." She sounded annoyed. "Mrs. Overbee is my trophy stepmother. She'll be along soon. She's getting her massage."

Miss Curro put out her cigarette and lit another one. I took a cue from her and lit one for myself. My last, I told myself.

"Is Missy your name?" I asked.

"It'll do. It's all that wetback greaser can remember. What's yours?"

"Manuel Garcia," I said just to piss her off. She sniffed and returned to reading her magazine.

Ramon returned with my drink and put it on a lace paper coaster on the round frosted glass table next to me. He handed Missy a shot glass full of a brown liquid, and she knocked it back and gave the glass back to Ramon, who vanished again.

"Isn't it a bit early?" I asked.

"Not in Mada—wherever," she said.

I took a small sip to see whether my demons from last night would return to churn my innards. An empty silver champagne bucket stood on its stand nearby. I kept it within reach in case the booze evicted the oatmeal and cantaloupe. The bright white porous patio deck looked like it would permanently stain from whatever came out of me.

To my surprise and delight, the bourbon was not only smooth, but it stayed down where it belonged and where it went immediately to work. Another swallow and I had that glow that comes only with the first drink. That's when you love everything and everybody. Another couple drinks and the love evaporates as you get drunk and depressed. If they could come up with a drink that keeps that buzz going, I'd buy stock in the company. Maybe Buford could advise me.

I remembered my resolve. Don't drink too much. I finished the drink, settled back, and Ramon was there again with a refill.

"What the hell," I said. "I'll quit some other time."

Missy looked up. "Quit what?"

About that time Buford came out onto the patio. He sat next to me, and Ramon was there right away with what looked like a tall glass of tomato juice. Buford stirred it with the celery stalk that stood up in the glass.

"Am I drinking alone?" I asked.

"Stoles and V8. Great for a hangover."

I made a mental note of that.

"Now," Buford said, "How did Rodney find where I live?"

"Your cell phone lives here too. He tracked it with the GPS."

"Holy shit. Technology. You can't escape it."

"Turn off the GPS when you don't need it," I said and showed him on my phone what Rodney had shown me.

"I take it you met Melissa." Buford gestured towards the lump in the chaise lounge. "My daughter, my pride and joy."

Melissa smiled at him, got up, and pulled her chaise lounge over next to Buford's.

The door from the house opened, and a young woman came out. Now this was more like in the detective novels. She was tall and slim with blonde hair and wearing designer sunglasses, elevated sandals, and a white terrycloth robe that fell open in the front to reveal a tiny black bikini on a hard body.

The bikini did its job, covering those parts of her that were not supposed to be seen in public and not much else. She might as well have been wearing two Band-Aids and a cork.

Just the kind of ten I never got. Even when I was young enough.

"Oh, great," Missy whispered to herself. "The princess." She rolled over on her chaise lounge so she wouldn't have to look at the vision of loveliness that had just joined us.

"You didn't tell me we expected company, Buford," the vision said. "I would have gotten, y'know, like dressed. Aren't you going to, like, introduce us?"

She still had that unmistakable teenaged girl dialect that everyone recognizes right away. "Didn't" was "didunt," and she bore the valley girl look. Her name had to be Muffy or Tiffany.

I tried to stand up, gentleman that I am.

"Don't like get up," she said.

Good thing. Getting up would be a problem. Buford's fine bourbon was beginning to take hold.

"Mr. Stanley Bentworth, this is my wife, Serena."

Not Muffy, but close enough.

"Pleased to meet you, Mr. Bentworth," she said. She sat on a chaise lounge, adjusted her robe for maximum exposure to the sun, making sure everyone was watching, and lowered herself to a reclining position.

"My pleasure, Mrs. Overbee."

She adjusted herself on the lounge and opened her robe to fully expose her body. The sun beat down through the glass ceiling.

"No matter how I try, I can't seem to, y'know, get a tan," she said.

"It won't work here," I said. "Greenhouse effect. UV light changes its waveform when it passes through glass."

"Huh?" she said.

"The words are too big, Mr. Bentworth," Missy said. "Serena, the tanning rays can't get in through a glass roof. That's why you're so pale. You have to go outside."

"But it's like cold out there," the valley girl answered. "Buford, sweetums, why don't you buy me a, y'know, tanning bed?"

Missy made a face like she was about to like, you know, puke.

Serena said to Buford, "Honey, how many have you like had? You know I don't want you drinking so early in the day."

"Thank you, darling," he said. "Ramon knows my limit."

Serena put her earphones on, adjusted her iPod, and tuned out the rest of us.

"Let's go in the study where we can talk," Buford said.

We got up, and left the ladies to themselves. Buford led me back into the house and into his large, paneled study. We sat in facing leather easy chairs.

I looked around the magnificent room and said, "So, when you kack, are you going to say, 'Rosebud'?"

His gun collection was prominently displayed in walnut cabinets with glass doors on two walls. It looked like he had at least one of every kind of handgun, rifle, and shotgun. I spotted an Uzi, an AK-47, an M-16 and two Thompson submachine guns.

"Those pieces fully automatic?" I asked, pointing at the assault weapons.

"They are," he said. Silly of me to ask.

"Now," he said, "what do you have to report?"

"First," I said, "This is what I know about you."

I recited all the facts we'd learned about Buford's past from the U.S. Marshals Service website. Buford sat quietly during the recitation.

When I finished he said, "Why did you need to learn all that?"

"You need to know how easy it can be to find out that kind of shit, is why. You're trying to stay out of sight and incognito, and an eighteen-year-old boy with orange hair learns everything there is to know about you in less than an hour. You don't think somebody else can do the same thing?"

"I see. About that murder rap, Stan, just so you know. The vic was a drug dealer. He was peddling his shit in my neighborhood in Philly. My daughter was one of his best customers. He didn't respond to conventional forms of persuasion, so I took a different tack. Problem solved. After that no one would sell to her. Got her into rehab, and she cleaned up."

"Did you do the deed yourself?"

"I took the fall. I'm telling you this just so you know that hits were not in my job description. The family had other resources for that."

"Understood," I said, relieved. At least I wouldn't have to worry about more than a broken arm or two if Buford and I ever had a falling out. Which I fully intended to avoid.

"What did you learn about my shake-down artist?" Buford said.

I took the note from my pocket and handed it to him.

"Name, address, phone number. Do you know him?"

"Mario Vitole. No. It sounds like he could be one of the boys, but I never heard that name."

"Out of town, maybe? Brought in to bring you down?"

"Not with blackmail. The family doesn't do it that way."

"You think he could be one of the feds?"

"Don't know. But I'll know soon enough. Or it won't matter."

"Wouldn't you rather go in armed with more knowledge?" I said.

"I'll be armed."

"But it's better to know what you're up against. Let's see what Rodney can come up with."

I pulled out my cell, put it on speaker and called Rodney.

"Where are you?" I asked.

"The Cheap Peeper Emporium."

"Jesus, kid. Don't get a sore wrist. You got your laptop with you?"

"Always."

"Can you get into the Marshals server again?"

"Yep. I'll have to get near a wi-fi router. There's a McDonald's near here. You see, without a signal—"

"Just do it. Go in there, and see what you can find out about Mario Vitole. See if the feds have anything on him. Call me when you have something."

"And if I can't find anything?"

"Call me either way."

Buford fidgeted in his easy chair. He downed the drink, and Ramon was there right away with a refill. That guy was always there when you needed him, Johnny-on-the-spot.

"He knows my limit," Buford said. "When I reach it, he stops bringing more."

"What if you insist?"

"Then he brings more." He took a sip of the new drink. "Why don't I go see this Vitole hump right now? I can probably straighten things out with a few well-chosen words. His main defense is that I'm not supposed to know who he is."

"Wouldn't you like to get your twenty grand back?"

"Sure. How would I do that?"

"Rodney."

"Jesus, is there anything that kid can't do?"

"He can't get money that isn't there. You go shoving Vitole around and he'll pull all the cash out of the account. Wait 'til we get the dough. Then you can let him know he's been busted."

"In more ways than one."

Buford had a look in his eye that I had not often seen in a man. Not an adversary to be reckoned with.

"Okay," he said. "We can wait. But not long."

My cell phone rang. Rodney was calling.

"Uncle Stanley, I have what you need."

"What'd you get?" I asked.

"Mario Vitole is a retired U.S. Marshal. His last duty station was the witness protection program in the New York corridor. He retired about a year ago."

"Vitole is a retired fed," I said to Buford. "He had access to your files when you were active. Now he's shaking you down I suppose to supplement his pension."

"Dirty rotten son of a bitch."

That's what I would have said.

"Might you know him by another name?" is what I did say.

"No. We didn't use nicknames. I knew my handlers by their real names, and they knew mine."

I spoke into the phone again.

"Great job, Rodney."

"That's not all, Uncle Stanley. I'm hacked into that OnlinePay account. What do you want me to do with it?"

"What's the balance?"

"About fifty grand."

I whistled. Vitole must have been shaking down other well-heeled protected witnesses. Or selling antiques on ebay.

"Stand by again." I turned again to Buford. "You want your twenty grand back?"

"Hell, yes."

"Got an offshore account somewhere that the feds can't see?"

"Of course."

"Get me the account numbers."

Buford got up and went to his desk, a huge mahogany behemoth with ornate carvings and inlays and not much clutter.

I said to Rodney, "I'm getting you a bank routing number and the client's account number. I want you to transfer twenty grand from Vitole's account into the client's account."

"Can do. I can get it all if you want. Put it in your account?"

I must admit I was tempted. "No. Just the twenty grand."

The feds might not know about Buford's account in Grand Cayman, or wherever, but my bank was in town with my name on file.

Buford returned with a slip of paper.

"Here they are."

I read the numbers to Rodney. I waited while his fingers did their tap dance on the laptop keyboard.

Then he said, "It's done."

"Great work, Rodney. I'll try to get you a bonus. Maybe a new shirt."

We hung up, and I said to Buford, "You got your twenty grand back, you got the name of the shakedown artist, and you know where he is. What else can I do for you?"

"I'm impressed. How did you get the twenty grand?"

"Rodney got it."

"Won't there be a trace to who got it and where it went?"

"Only if the guy complains. And Rodney doesn't leave a clean trail in cyberspace. What's the asshole going to tell the cops, anyway? 'I blackmailed a guy, and he hacked my account and took the money back'?"

"Good point."

Buford handed me an envelope.

"There's ten grand in there."

He sure knew how to get a guy's attention.

"That puts you on retainer for a month, weekends off," he said. "I don't have anything for you to do right now, but something will come up. I want you standing by while I get to Mr. Vitole before he realizes we got to him."

I put the envelope in my jacket pocket. Ten grand. Willa would be ecstatic.

"Have you considered turning Vitole in to the feds and letting them handle it?"

"I have not. I do my own housecleaning."

"How about if I go talk to him? Explain what we have on him and that we'll rat him out to his former employer if he doesn't back down. I think him knowing that we know should be enough."

"What if he doesn't go for it?"

"Then do it your way."

"Let Mr. Bentworth try, Daddy," Missy said. She was standing in the doorway. She must have heard everything. "I don't want you to get hurt. Or you can send Sanford to do it."

"Who's Sanford?" I asked Buford.

"Sometimes he's my lawyer."

Sometimes? How can you be a part-time lawyer? What do you do the rest of the time? Repossess pacemakers?

"Well, ask him. Whatever you do might have legal consequences. I don't want Rodney and me on anybody's accessories list. Before or after the fact."

"A pragmatist," Buford said.

"Every time," I said.

"I hate pragmatists," he said. "Okay, make a call on him. Let me know how it turns out."

Missy nodded her approval of our plan.

Chapter 6

I enjoyed a pleasant drive on a thoroughfare to the south, going across the river and under the Interstate. It was lunch time. I stopped at a fast food drive-through and got a burger and fries. With the hangover gone, the thought of all that grease and gristle didn't bother me. I got back on the road and ate while I drove.

Mario Vitole's house was a rambler in a suburban subdivision. Nothing fancy, but nice. A new Buick was parked in the carport, and the lawn was well-tended. A cute but tacky sign on the lawn announced to the world that the house was the dwelling of Mario and Stella Vitole.

I parked across the street and a few houses down. My car had tinted windows so, unless someone looked closely, they couldn't tell that I was in there. I took my digital Nikon camera from the glove box, put the long range lens in, and waited.

This was routine for me, the same kind of surveillance I did on cheating spouses. Only this time, instead of catching an indiscretion, I wanted to chart the target's movements to see where he went and what he did. I'd choose a way to confront him based on that.

At about two o'clock, a man came out of the house. He was about sixty-five, with a medium height and build, and curly black hair with streaks of white. Tan and good-looking for an old guy. I rolled down the window and snapped a picture of him. He walked up the sidewalk to the residence two houses away. I took pictures. He went in the front door. Odd. He didn't knock, just went in.

I drove up a few yards to just across from the doorway of the house where he went in.

About an hour later the door opened. I started snapping. He came to the doorway, and a woman came along behind. She was wearing a robe. He kissed her, came out, and returned to his own house. I took more pictures. I wrote down the neighbor's house number. Then I called Rodney.

"Rodney, find me the name of whoever lives at 512 Cherokee Avenue."

Rodney tapped and clicked. After about a minute of that, he said, "William Sproles. Do you need more information?"

"Can you get his wife's name?"

Tap, tap, click, click. "Marsha. Anything else?"

"Find out what you can about them."

I called Vitole.

"Mr. Vitole, I need to speak with you privately."

"About what? Who is this?"

"This is about one of the former clients in witness protection."

"I retired. You must want somebody else."

"This is about Anthony Curro, also known as Buford Overbee."

The line got quiet for a moment. Then, "Who is this?"

"We need to speak alone," I said. "I'm parked just up the street. Where's a good place nearby to meet?"

"You want to come to the house?"

"Anybody else there?"

"No. I'm alone," he said. "My wife won't be home until about six."

"Okay. Keep in mind, this is just a meeting. An exchange of information. I come in peace." I smiled at the Captain Kirk reference. "I expect to be likewise received. If not, your next visitor won't be so peaceful. Understood?"

"Understood." So far my usual bluff was working.

He was waiting in the doorway when I pulled up. He had changed into shorts, a T-shirt, and flip-flops. I got out of my car and walked up the sidewalk towards him. He retreated into the house and waved me in.

He walked ahead of me down a hallway. He looked back to size me up. This was where my bluff really needed to work. Not only am I not tough, I don't look tough.

The house was tastelessly decorated with pile carpeting, red flock wallpaper, and etched mirror tiles. New simulated antiques decorated the entranceway, and the furniture and wall hangings were new too, every schlock style imaginable, nothing matching, nothing coordinated. But much nicer than my place, you can be sure.

He led me into the living room and pointed to a chair. I sat and he plopped on a sofa across from me.

"You want a beer or something?"

"No, thanks."

"So, what's this about Overbee?"

"Someone's been shaking him down."

He paused. "Really?" His mock surprise was not well-delivered, given what I already knew. "How?"

"They're threatening to out him with his clients and with the mob."

"No shit. You understand, I was not his handler. I never met the guy." He was getting jumpy.

"I know. But you know all the major players in the Marshals Service. Maybe you can get the word out."

"What word?"

"We traced the blackmailer's e-mail address to his OnlinePay account and hacked into the account."

His face got white.

"We recovered the twenty grand Overbee already paid the blackmailer. Next time the blackmailer signs on, he'll be a lot poorer."

Vitole started looking around as if he needed to check something. He took a gulp of his beer.

I continued. "It's a short jump from the account to its owner. If the blackmailer persists in his extortion, we will make that jump and turn our records over to the feds."

I watched for his reaction to that. His face turned red.

"If that doesn't bring it to a stop," I said, "Mr. Overbee and his business associates will make a personal call on the blackmailer. In fact, that's what he wanted to do right off the bat, but I talked him out of it. I think we can safely say that whoever it is, he's still walking around thanks to my intervention."

You wouldn't expect a retired U.S. Marshal to be that easily intimidated, but Vitole looked like he was about to crap his shorts.

Now for the clincher. "If this doesn't go down right, if the blackmailer puts any more of a squeeze on, the shit hits the fan."

I paused to let the indirect threat sink in. Vitole bit his lower lip and ran his hand across his mouth like a junkie needing a fix. His eyes darted from side to side, and he squirmed on the sofa.

"Why do you think I'd know who it is?" he asked.

"Witness protection is a small team. It's got to be one of your former colleagues, probably also retired like yourself. Nobody else has access to the files to know who to target. So, try to pass the word along. And we can bring this matter to a peaceful close."

I said a polite goodbye, went out to my car, and called Buford.

"I think he's convinced," I said.

"He better be."

"But if not, I've got leverage. He's fooling around with his neighbor's wife. I'll e-mail you the evidence when I get back to the office."

I drove around the block and parked between Vitole's house and the Sproles's so I could watch both. At about six o'clock, Vitole's wife came home from wherever she had spent the day and parked her Toyota next to his Buick. I took a couple pictures of her going from the car to the house. Not a pretty woman, she was overweight with gray hair and looked to be in her late fifties or early sixties. She went in the house.

A short time later, a car pulled into the Sproles residence. A man got out and went into the house. He was middle-aged and looked like the couch potato type. I got more pictures. Then I headed back to the office.

Chapter 7

I always have trouble finding my cell phone when it rings in the car and I'm driving. I've usually tossed it on the passenger's seat because I can't hear it in my pocket over the sound of the engine. Then it gets lost among the other trash on the seat. Old fast food bags, scribbled notes and directions on bar napkins from months before, gas receipts, my GPS, and the like. By the time I find the cell phone, the caller has given up.

This time I found it only because I had just used it to call Vitole. Amanda was calling.

"What's up, sis?"

She was crying.

"Stanley, I don't know what to do."

That was her usual complaint when she couldn't figure something out. "About what?" I asked.

"About Jeremy."

"Who's that?"

"The Army Captain I've been going out with."

"Oh, yeah. Captain Jeremy. Didn't you dump him?"

"I tried. He won't accept it. He keeps calling, and today he hung around my office all morning. I'm afraid I'll lose my job. The last thing he said was that he'd come to my house this evening."

"Did you tell him you'd call his wife?"

"He said he didn't care. She's going to leave him anyway."

"Did you say you'd report him to his Commanding Officer?"

"He doesn't care about that either. He has his twenty years in and is about to retire."

Twenty in and still a Captain. This guy must be a real piece of work.

"What do I do?" she asked.

"Well, given that he's about to split up with his wife, might you still want to see him?"

"No, Stanley. I saw his ugly side today. He didn't take it too well when I told him I had a private investigator looking into him and found out he was married. He scared me."

"Did he touch you?"

"He followed me down the hall, cornered me outside the ladies room, yelled at me, and pushed me so hard I sat on the floor."

That got my slow burn going. It takes a lot, but messing with my family is one of the ways.

"When do you expect him?" I asked.

"Tonight some time after supper."

"Okay. To start, let's post Rodney there wearing his taco shirt. I'll explain to him. If that doesn't discourage the Captain, I'll take over. Don't worry. I'll be parked around the corner from your place. What's he look like?"

"Sandy hair. Fortyish. Crew cut. Glasses. Average size. Kind of cute."

Younger than me and probably in better shape. Hell, my grandmother's in better shape, and she's been dead for ten years. I'd need an edge, an equalizer. Time to get old Roscoe out of the safe.

Yeah, that's right, I named my .38 Roscoe. They don't pay me for my imagination.

I drove to my office building and climbed the stairs. It was late afternoon. I stopped at Willa's desk, tossed Buford's envelope there, and went into my office. She gave out with a war whoop when she opened the package.

Rodney was already back from the Cheap Peeper Emporium. He was at my desk again.

"When you gonna get me my own desk," he asked.

"Where would we put it? In the men's room?"

"In here. There's room."

"No, there's not."

I turned on the Nikon and paged through the images to the ones with Vitole and Marsha Sproles.

"Download these pictures to your laptop and e-mail them to Buford Overbee."

He got out a cable to connect the camera to the laptop.

"Did you find out anything about the Sproles family?" I asked.

"Not much. They moved into the neighborhood a couple years ago. I couldn't find where they came from."

"One other thing unrelated. See if you can hack into the Army computers and find out what you can about Captain Pugh. Do it in the outer office. I need some privacy."

He took the camera, cable, and laptop and left.

"Close the door," I said.

I got my pistol out of the safe and checked the cylinder. Six cartridges. I don't know why I checked. I'd loaded it when I first got it several years ago and had never fired it. But old habits and all that.

I took my private detective's gold shield from my wallet and pinned it to the holster. From a distance it looked just like a Delbert Falls detective's shield, which was why I had ordered this particular model from the Internet badge and uniform store. Thirty bucks and authentic-looking. But its golden shine notwithstanding, it signified nothing more than to impress gullible clients and people you want to question. Flash it, and people open up. For all the clout it gave me, I could have gotten it from a Cracker Jack box. And saved the thirty bucks.

I clipped the holster to my belt in front just under my jacket. Then I called Rodney back in.

"The Captain is coming to your mom's house tonight," I said. "I want you there. When he comes to the door, speed dial my cell and leave your phone on the table next to the door. I want to hear everything that goes down."

"What happens if he gets rough, Uncle Stanley?"

"I won't be far away. Be as nasal, whiny, and obnoxious as you can be. In other words, be yourself. If he does get rough, make sure I hear it."

Rodney nodded.

"Keep in mind you're protecting your mother," I said.

"Yep."

I didn't tell Rodney that the Captain had knocked Amanda down. I wasn't sure what he would do. Might get himself hurt. So might I. But I was going to do something. Not sure what, but something.

"What did you learn about the Captain?" I asked.

"Mentally unstable. A history of paranoia and obsessive-compulsive disorder. Manic depressive, too. A real mess. He's on the verge of being discharged on a section eight, whatever that is."

"That's when they boot you out of the service because you're nuts," I said. "Get over to the house and get ready. Your mom is expecting you. This ought to be interesting."

I said earlier that I am not tough. That's true. But I am a good bluffer and an even better actor. My young years as an undercover cop had taught me that. I had been a good undercover cop. The bad guys never suspected I was a cop. I didn't look like one. I could blend in as the guy who did whatever he was told.

But when the situation called for it, I could act tough. Especially with backup.

Tonight I'd get a chance to revisit those old skills. I started to get together what I'd need.

Chapter 8

The south side of Delbert Falls was residential. Small single-family houses and inexpensive apartments west of the tracks, and the better homes for the upper middle class on tree-lined lanes on the east side.

Amanda's neighborhood was south of my office on the west side past the Interstate. Sunset had started and it would be dark soon. I pulled up to the curb near the house and parked where I could see her front door. I hoped I wouldn't have to wait in the car for long. It was going to be cold. She lived in a small, one-story house in a row of identical houses, nothing fancy. My cell phone rang.

"You out there, Uncle Stanley?"

"Yep, just got here."

"Mom is nervous."

"Put her on. And bring me your baseball bat."

Amanda came on. "Stanley—"

"Don't worry, Mandy. Stay back, and let Rodney handle it. I've told him what to do. When your boyfriend comes out, I'll take it from there."

"He's not my boyfriend."

"Right. Keep thinking that thought."

I hung up, and Rodney was at my car with the ball bat right away. I took it, and he went back into the house. I lit a cigarette. This would be my last one. Or my last pack. They were expensive. I'd have to finish the pack. Can't let them go to waste.

Waiting and watching from my car reminded me of countless stakeouts, except that tonight I didn't have coffee and doughnuts. Buford's booze had worn off. I had a pint of Old Forester in the glove compartment for emergencies in case of snake bite, so I took it out, looked around for a snake, didn't see one, and took a swig. No more than one, though, I told myself. I needed my wits about me. So I took another swig. I'm weak. So sue me.

At about seven, a silver BMW pulled up in front of Amanda's house. A fellow fitting Jeremy's description got out, went to the door, and rang the doorbell.

My cell phone buzzed. This time I found it right away on top of the trash that decorated my front seat. I picked it up.

"He's here, Uncle Stanley."

"Okay. You know what to do."

Rodney opened the door and said. "What do you want?"

I could hear the exchange on my cell phone.

"I want to talk to your mother."

"She doesn't want to talk to you."

"Get out of the way, kid."

"Or what?"

"Or maybe I move you out of the way."

With that I was out of my car and headed for the front door carrying the ball bat.

The Captain raised his voice. "Amanda! Get out here. We need to talk."

Amanda's voice came from inside the house. "Go away, Jeremy. I don't want to see you."

I was just behind Jeremy when he started to shove Rodney aside and push his way into the house. He didn't see me coming. I swung the bat with all my might, hitting him across both calves. He yelled and went down sideways off the stoop into the bushes beside the door.

"What the fuck—?" he said.

"Stay down," I said. "Stay where you are."

He sized me up from his position on the ground.

"Says who?" he said.

"Captain, you're pretty good at pushing women and helpless teen-aged boys around. How are you when you're up against a man?"

He started to get up to show me, but I hit him in the ribs with the bat. Hard enough to hurt but not hard enough to break anything. He fell back, holding his side, then rose again and braced himself to spring. I let my jacket fall open so that the holstered pistol and shield were in clear view. He stopped and sank back down.

"So she called the cops," he said.

"No, asshole, she called her big brother. You see, I take a dim view of people pushing my sister around. A very dim view. You ever lay another hand on her, and you'll be taking a dim view too. The dimmest. From inside a shallow grave."

"Are you threatening me?"

"Gee," I said to Rodney. "I must not have done it right. Here he is, on the ground, hugging his rib cage, big assed bruises on his legs, maybe a cracked rib, me standing over him with a baseball bat, and him asking if I'm threatening him." I turned to Jeremy. "Goddamn right I'm threatening you, asshole! Come around here again, and you get more of the same. Is there any part of that that isn't clear?"

This was a little more direct than the approach I'd taken with Vitole. I liked it better this way.

Amanda called from inside the house, "Stanley, make him go away."

Terrific. Now he has my name.

As I said earlier, I'm not a tough guy, but I do have balls. Comes from years working homicide and robbery. You always had backup. A murder cop was seldom in real danger. All the action had already happened. They called us in to clean it up. I was out on my own now, no help, no backup, but the balls were still in place and working. It felt good. But if he'd tried to jump me, I would have had to shoot him. Then there'd be paperwork.

"Stay on the ground," I said, hoping he'd agree.

I looked fondly at the Louisville Slugger in my grip. Rodney and I used to play flies and grounders with it on the vacant lot behind the house when he was younger. And when I was younger too. Now the old Slugger was being put to professional use, and I was about to improve my batting average.

I walked over to the silver Beamer and broke one headlight. Then I broke the passenger's side of the windshield. Then a tail-light. For the final out I banged a good-sized dent in the passenger's side door. Then I walked back to the house and handed the bat to Rodney. The Captain was still on the ground staring first at me then at his car.

"I left you enough to see your way home," I told the Captain. "Make sure you never see your way back. I find you here again, it's your head, legs, ribs, anything I can reach, instead of that pussy Beamer. And no more mister nice guy. Next time I break something. Now get the fuck out of here."

He pulled himself to his feet, limped over to his car, hugging his ribs and glaring at me all the way, and got in. He rolled the passenger window down half way, which got caught up in the damage I'd done, and called out, "You haven't heard the last of this." Then he drove away.

Probably true. I went inside.

"If you hear from him again, Amanda, call me. Keep your door locked and don't let him in."

"I will. Thanks, Stanley." She gave me a hug, which made it all worth while.

"What's his job with the Army?" I asked.

"Something to do with intelligence," she said.

Oh, great. Now I'm certain to hear from him again.

"Hey, Uncle Stanley," Rodney said, "I ain't no helpless teen-age boy. I could have taken him myself."

"When you tell this story at school, you can tell it that way."

"I don't go to school."

"You should."

The booze was wearing off. I went home and went straight to bed.

Chapter 9

The alarm clock woke me at seven thirty. No hangover. That was pleasant. I could get used to that. With a shower and shave, dressed and out the door, I was on my way to work.

An olive drab Chevy with official white markings fell in behind me. I couldn't make out the lettering, but I could guess. Captain Pugh had sent some payback. I'm not sure where he got my home address. I could see two large men in Army uniforms in the front seat of the car. The driver was young, big, and had a serious look about him. The other one was in the shadows.

I drove north under the Interstate and to the police station and pulled into a parking space marked "Official Police Vehicles Only." The olive drab Chevy sped away.

I didn't get out. I backed out of the parking space just as a uniform was walking over to tell me I couldn't park there. I smiled and waved at him and drove to my office.

Willa wasn't in yet. She must've stopped at the bank to deposit our windfall. I was right. I settled in at my desk, and she came in, smiling.

"Good morning, boss man," she said, taking off her coat and tossing a deposit slip on her desk. "The Bentworth Detective Agency is in the black for the first time I can remember. All caught up on our bills, and my back salary is paid in full at last."

"Anything left?"

"Some."

"How much?"

"I'm not going to tell you. You'd just spend it."

"That I would."

"Your paycheck is in your desk drawer. Spend that."

I opened the drawer and looked at the check.

"What? I get a pay cut?"

"Times are tough, boss man. There's a recession on. Got to tighten our belts. We all have to pitch in and do our part."

You'd have thought she was selling war bonds.

I left the office and went to Ray's. Bunny was there with a disappointed look on her face.

"Where were you last night?" she said.

"Sleeping off a fight."

"A fight?"

"Yeah. A guy's been pestering Amanda. Now he's not."

"You look better than yesterday. Fighting must be better for you than drinking. I'll get your breakfast."

She went into the kitchen and returned with the usual bacon, eggs, and all that.

"You're perfect, Bunny. I need a cholesterol fix."

"Thanks, Stan. You're looking better too. So, what do you think? Want to get back together?"

"Still thinking about it."

"I won't mention it again," she said. "I'm not used to rejection."

"It gets harder to take and more frequent as you get older," I said before I could stop myself.

She turned with a flip and left to take care of other customers. I ate alone, glad for the solitude. I had several things on my mind. What was I to do about Jeremy and the Gestapo twins? Would Vitole lay off Buford? Would Rodney's illegal money transfer come back to haunt me? And, of course, there was Bunny. What was I going to do about Bunny?

This pile of complications made looking for bail jumpers and cheating husbands feel like the good old days.

I finished breakfast and went back to the office. I went into the inner office, sat in my chair, and dozed off.

After a while Willa came to the door, "Somebody's here to see you."

I came awake and sat forward. "Who?"

"Bill Penrod."

I stood up and rubbed my eyes as Penrod came in.

"Hello, Stan."

"Come in, Bill," I said. "Sit down. Good to see you. What does Delbert Falls's finest need this morning?"

He looked at his watch. "It's afternoon."

Bill had been my shift supervisor when I was in homicide. We were close friends and had worked well together, partnering on many cases. Sometimes he was primary, sometimes I was. We had a good closure rate, an unbeatable team. I was good at finding witnesses and suspects, and Bill was the interrogator. He could've wrangled a confession out of O.J. We were both good at finding clues and gathering information. Breaking up our team was the Lieutenant's biggest mistake, although he would never admit it.

He plopped in the chair in front of the desk. His bulk filled it up. He took out a handkerchief and wiped his brow. Bill would have perspired at the North Pole.

"Smoke in here?"

"Yep."

"Can't smoke in the squad room," he said. "Have to go to a designated area outside. They should know what that costs the city in lost manpower. At any given time, half the shift's out there."

"Shift happens." I pushed the ash tray across to him. He lit a cigarette with the old Ronson lighter that I'd always coveted, snapped it shut, and took a drag.

I said for the thousandth time, "If you ever quit smoking, I want that lighter."

He grunted and looked like he was enjoying the smoke. I wished I wasn't trying to quit. I still had a couple in my pack. I lit one up. Just to be sociable.

"We got a guy in custody says he talks only to you, Stan, He already lawyered up."

"Who is it?"

"Buford Overbee."

Things just got more complicated. It looked like I might just earn out that ten grand retainer.

"What did he do?"

"We like him for a murder this morning. A retired fed named Mario Vitole. What can you tell us?"

My mind was spinning at ten thousand revs per minute. What had gone wrong? Did Vitole fail to understand my warning? Did he really think we didn't know he had been the blackmailer?

"Not much. I did some work for Overbee not long ago."

"I know. I sent him to you. Some kind of vague missing person situation."

"Same guy."

"What was the case?"

"I'm still on retainer with Overbee, Bill. I'll have to talk to him before I can talk to you about that. But I don't think my case is related to this." A little white lie. They were related.

"Stan, you know the drill. It's murder. P.I. to client privilege doesn't work here."

"I know," I said. Bill didn't need to tell me how it works. It hadn't been that long ago that I was on his side of the table.

"You know something, you got to tell me," he said. "I don't want to have to file an obstruction charge against you."

"I don't want you to."

"Some judge will put your sorry ass in the clink with a contempt violation if you dummy up. And I'm the only one on my side who'll give a shit what happens to you."

"Understood. I'll spill. But can you cut me a little slack until I talk to Overbee? He isn't going anywhere, and the vic won't get any deader."

"I guess I can do that since it's you. But don't tell the Lieutenant. He doesn't love you like I do."

"Thanks. What can you tell me about the case?"

"A neighbor found the body late this morning in the street a couple doors from his house. He had a bullet in his brain. Small caliber, from the front between his eyes, no GSR, no exit wound. His nose had been recently rearranged."

"Which way from his house?" I was thinking about Marsha Sproles and a jealous husband.

"North."

Bingo! He had gotten bumped in front of his girl friend's house. I figured I'd hang onto that piece of knowledge until it could help.

"Who was the neighbor who found him?"

He looked at his notepad. "Marsha Sproles."

The girlfriend found the body. I wondered whether there was any significance to that.

"Did the vic have any connection with the mob?"

"He worked witness protection before he retired."

"Well, that's sure a connection. You need to look into all his cases from before he retired."

"I got somebody on that. The feds are cooperating. Up to a point. For once, they don't want jurisdiction. But they're not willing to open their books."

"Not even for one of their own?"

"Retired. Second-class citizen. It's our case."

"Interesting. Anyway, what makes you like a renowned financier more than the mob?"

"The vic's wife. One night when Overbee was mentioned on the news, Vitole told her they were about to score big on him, something about a better retirement plan."

"Score how?"

"She didn't know."

"That's not much for an arrest warrant."

"The judge saw it our way. Overbee can't account for his whereabouts, so no alibi; a witness saw his car at the vic's house early this morning; he has a wall full of guns hanging in his study; and he owns a private jet, making him a flight risk."

"Still sounds circumstantial to me. Weak. How'd the witness know it was Overbee's car?"

"She didn't. We made the connection."

"How?"

"Christ, Stan. It's a fucking white Rolls Royce. How many of them you see around here?"

"Point taken. Still not on solid ground, though."

Penrod nodded. The case was shaky and he knew it. "The M.E. will get the bullet out of the vic's noggin, and the lab can see if it matches one of Overbee's guns. We confiscated all the small caliber pieces. I'm betting we get a match."

"I'm betting you don't." Buford was too smart to use a personal gun and then keep it. If he shot Vitole, the gun was at the bottom of the river.

"That, and a confession ought to close it," Penrod said.

"Good luck on that," I said.

"Well, I'm pretty good in the room."

He was. The "room" was what we called homicide's interrogation room. Many cases were closed in the room.

"But you don't know Overbee," I said. "Hard case. If he did it, he won't give it up. Did you meet his wife?"

"Yes. Wow." He whistled a quiet low tone.

"Uh huh. And his daughter?"

"Didn't know he had one. What's she like?"

"Not wow. But devoted to Daddy."

"The wife didn't mention her."

I gave an all-knowing shrug. Bill responded in kind.

"From what I've seen," I said, "they're not on the best of terms."

"The daughter live there?"

"I think so."

"I'll question her too. When can you talk to Overbee?"

I wanted that talk more than Bill did. I wanted to find out what happened and maybe even keep the meter running a ways past his ten grand retainer.

"Any time. Let me know."

"I'll call his lawyer. He wants to be there. Maybe tomorrow."

"Call me when you know."

"I will." Penrod looked me square in the eye. "Then I expect full disclosure."

"I know." I also knew that Bill Penrod wouldn't let up on me. I'd have to spill most of it.

Penrod started to get up to leave. Then I said, "Does the press have the story yet?"

He sat back down.

"Not yet."

"You got mug shots?"

"Of course." His tone said that I shouldn't have had to ask.

"Get yourself copies," I told him. "You can sell them to one of the tabloids before the other news hawks get them. They'd all kill to get a photo of the elusive Buford Overbee."

Penrod laughed. "Might just do that, Stan. Then I can retire. Need a partner?"

I leaned back in my chair and crossed my arms. The idea of partnering with Bill Penrod again was beyond my wildest hopes. If only the business would support it.

"I wish," was all I could say. "Seriously, about the mug shots. The mob's been looking for him for years. He pled out a murder rap with a deal that let him walk in exchange for testifying. They don't know his name or where he is. You let his picture get out, and his life isn't worth a rusty Al Gore campaign button."

"I'll pass it on," Penrod said.

Chapter 10

The next morning I stopped at McDonald's and got coffee and a sausage biscuit. Then I went directly to the police station. My army pals were on my tail again. They knew where I lived. I hoped they'd think I was a cop. So far, both times they'd tailed me, I'd gone to the police station. When I pulled into the parking lot this morning they sped off just as they'd done the previous time.

Whatever they had in mind, they obviously didn't want to go into action here. Or at the McDonald's drive-through. Too many cops here, too many witnesses there. It occurred to me that I might have to start carrying Roscoe. The last thing I wanted to do, though, was shoot an army spook. That would be some serious paperwork.

Maybe they were just trying to scare me off so I wouldn't get on Jeremy's case if he bothered Amanda again. Fat chance. I might be scared, but I wouldn't be scared off.

I went into the station. The desk sergeant sent me to the interrogation room where Buford was waiting. He sat on the far side of the table where suspects were interrogated. A thin, greasy-looking guy in a cheap, ill-fitting black suit stood against the wall.

"Stan, this is Sanford, my legal advisor," Buford said, indicating the skinny guy.

Sanford nodded and I nodded back. He did not look like a lawyer. He looked more like a street hustler, a pimp. The cheap suit didn't fit him because it wasn't tailor-made and he was as thin as a barbecue skewer. The pants were baggy and the jacket hung down off his shoulders. A thick watch chain dangling to the floor would have completed the fifties zoot suit persona, but he didn't have one.

"Did you confess yet?" I asked Buford. He smiled and shook his head.

I told them what Penrod had told me about what he had on Buford so far. Sanford shrugged it off.

"Not much to go on," he said.

"A witness seeing my car there, that's kind of incriminating," Buford said.

I looked Sanford up and down. He returned the examination. Not a guy to mess with. I needed him out of there.

"Buford, Sanford ought to wait out there," I said, indicating the door.

"I stay," Sanford said.

"We need someone out there making sure they're not listening to what we say," I said.

"I'm Mr. Overbee's counselor, Bentworth. They can't listen in. Attorney-client privilege."

"I don't know how much you know about police work, Mr. Sanford, but I used to be a detective here. We listened to everything. We couldn't always use it in court, but sometimes it told us whether we were on the right track, or what track to get on, and shit like that."

"Bullshit," he said. "That violates a suspect's constitutional right to counsel," Sanford said.

"So it does," I said.

"I'm staying," he said again.

"Buford," I said. "Unless Sanford knows everything there is to know about this case, you need to get him the fuck out of here. I need to be able to talk openly, and so do you."

"Wait out there," Buford said to Sanford.

Sanford shrugged and headed for the door without objection.

"Wait in the little cubicle on the other side of that mirror," I said. "That's the only place they can eavesdrop. They won't try it if you're there."

"How do you know I won't listen?"

"You don't know where the switch is."

Sanford left.

When he was gone, I said, "He doesn't look happy."

"He never looks happy. Even when he's happy."

I waited until Sanford had time to be clear of the room and said, "Buford, did you shoot Vitole?"

"No." He shook his head, and I believed him.

"Do you know who did?"

"No."

"You know how bad it looks, don't you? First you didn't know who was shaking you down. Then you did. Then you go to see him. Then he gets whacked."

"I know how bad it looks."

I leaned forward on the table. He leaned back.

"Tell me everything that happened after I called you," I said.

"That evening I checked my e-mail. There was a message saying I better put the twenty grand back or he'd call the newspapers."

Man, that guy Vitole had balls. I as much as told him we'd come after the blackmailer if that happened.

"Shit," I said. "I should have told him we knew it was him. I tried to dance around to let him get out of it gracefully. I guess I gave him credit for more smarts than he had. What did you do."

Buford got up and walked over to the mirror. He looked at himself and then came back to the table and stood alongside it.

"The next morning I took a drive to his house. When he opened the door, I punched him square in the face."

"I bet that got his attention."

"It did. I told him that if I heard anything more from him about money, I'd ruin his life."

"Which you are able to do."

"I am. I had a print of one of the pictures you took of him kissing his neighbor's wife. I tossed it at him and told him that if he made the slightest trouble, I'd send the picture to his old lady and the girl friend's husband."

"The blackmailee blackmailing the blackmailer. Nice twist."

"I told him that if that didn't work, I'd kill him. Then I went home. He was alive last I saw him. Had a sore beezer, but it was still breathing."

"I wonder if his old lady found that picture," I said.

He sat down again.

I continued. "Okay. Some things you should know. I had to tell the cops that the mob is looking for you."

"Why?"

"To keep them from releasing your mug shot to the press."

"Shit. I didn't think of that."

I always like it when I think of something that nobody else thinks of. Makes me look smart. I need all the help I can get.

"I don't know whether the cops'll hold your picture back, but I had to try. Also, the other bad news. I'm going to have to tell Penrod what I know about the case. Within limits. Otherwise he'll charge me with obstruction. I have to give him enough to satisfy him."

Buford nodded his approval. "I guess that's okay. Got to keep you on the street."

"Now. How do you want me to proceed?"

He leaned forward again and looked me squarely in the eye. "You were homicide," he said. "You said you closed cases. Close this one. Find out who the fuck did it."

Great. The meter would keep running.

"No matter who it is?" I asked.

"Why would I give a shit who it is?"

I'd save that one for later.

"Have they charged you?"

"They have."

"Arraigned?"

"No. Later today."

"Okay. The prosecution will ask for remand. Your lawyer will ask for recognizance. With luck it'll be something in between."

It was time to voice my concern about Sanford.

"I'll leave the choice of lawyers up to you, Buford, but I think you need to get a better-looking lawyer. One that doesn't look like a two-bit gangster in a zoot suit."

"I'll have to. Sanford is my chauffer, bodyguard, and right-hand man."

"I can't imagine you needing a bodyguard, and I can't imagine him being one," I said.

"Looks can be deceiving."

"Yours or his?"

"Both. Sanford was a lawyer for the mob, but got disbarred. Kind of short on ethics and it caught up with him."

All of a sudden I liked Sanford a lot more. "I know how that goes."

"He came with me when I left the family. Very loyal, very protective."

Buford adjusted his huge frame in the small metal folding chair. "So anyway, how do I keep my mug out of the newsreels?"

"Avoid cameras. When word gets out you're in here, the press'll be all over this place like stretch marks on a ninth-street lap dancer. When the cops take you between the jail and the courthouse, cover your face with your coat. Defendants do that all the time. That might keep your pretty face off the six o'clock news."

I tapped on the mirror and signaled for Sanford to come in. He did and I explained that I would be investigating the murder and trying to clear his boss. Buford told him to give me whatever help I needed. Sanford grunted his assent.

I left the two of them there and went down to Bill Penrod's desk in the squad room. The desk was pushed up against a column in the middle of the squad room. The desk was wider than the column, so things on the desk fell onto the floor on either side of the column. I could swear that there was stuff still on the floor from when I worked next to him years ago.

"Okay, Stan. Let's have it."

I told him the whole story, who Overbee was, why Vitole was blackmailing him, and that Vitole was banging Marsha Sproles.

"Bill, Overbee asked me to look into the murder and try to find out who did it."

"We already have a perp, Stan. Overbee did it. One of his guns is a match for the slug the ME took out of Vitole's brain."

"That doesn't make sense, Bill. Why would a major player like Overbee bump some guy then hang the piece back on the wall with his collection?"

"It wasn't on the wall. It was somewhere else."

"Where?"

"In the trunk of his car."

That sounded downright stupid to me. Buford would not have hidden a gun in his car.

"Registered to Overbee?"

"No. All his guns are unregistered."

"How do you know it was his?"

"Because of where we found it."

My first thought was Sanford. I didn't know how stupid he might be.

"Did you check out his chauffer?"

"You mean his lawyer?" Penrod laughed. "Yeah, we did. He has an alibi."

"This has to be some kind of frame-up."

"I know you want to believe that, Stan, but you know how it goes. We got this one practically closed. The guy is a former wise guy. Tough. With a lot to lose if his cover is exposed. And he was seen there the morning of the murder. Motive, means, opportunity."

The holy trinity of a murder investigation. Find someone who has all three, and most times you've found your killer.

"Before you declare it closed, Bill, keep in mind the neighbor, Sproles. He had a motive. Vitole was doing his wife and got whacked in front of their house. And Vitole's wife too. He was cheating on her. You got more than enough likely suspects."

Bill wouldn't budge.

"But then there's the gun," he said. "I can't see any way to link it to anyone else. I'm going into the room now with this new piece of evidence and get my confession.

"Let me know if you get it. Otherwise, I have work to do."

I hoped he didn't get it. The meter would stop running.

"Just stay out of our way, Stan."

"How can I be in your way if you closed the case? You won't be out there investigating any more."

"Good point. But I know you. Where there's a way, you'll be in it."

Chapter 11

I left the police station and drove to my office. I didn't see the olive-drab Chevy anywhere on my route. Captain Jeremy was sure to want his payback for the ass-kicking I'd given him and his car. I wasn't sure which I'd enjoyed more, hitting him with the baseball bat or that ostentatious Beamer.

I parked on a side street and walked into the alley to go in the back entrance to the building.

The next thing I knew, one of the two Army goons was walking towards me from the far end of the alley. I looked behind me for a place to run. The other one was coming from the other end. I almost shit my pants. Here I was, surrounded by muscle bearing down on me, and Roscoe was safely stored three stories up. Maybe it was for the best. I might have shot a couple soldiers. Paperwork.

I got to the doorway before they got to me and tried to open the door. Locked. I had a key, and I fumbled for it. Before I could get it out, they were on me.

One of them spun me around and pinned my arms behind me. The other one faced me. They were both bigger, stronger, and younger. Other than for that, I was okay.

"Stanley Bentworth, I presume," he said. "Phony cop. Likes to beat up on our Captain."

The other one said, "The Captain checked up on you, Stanley. Found out you aren't a cop. Found out what you are, asshole. Now we're going to show you what happens to someone who fucks with our people."

"You guys got no beef with me," I said. I struggled to get free. The last thing I wanted was to be kicked around by two healthy

71

soldiers. "Your boss likes to beat up on women and kids. Guys like that give the Army a bad name."

"Won't work, pal."

I kept struggling but it didn't help. "Then tell the son-of-a-bitch this," I said. "The next time I see him will be the worst day in his miserable fucking life."

I didn't think the bluff would deter them from their mission, but it was worth a try.

I could see it now, them saying, "You know, you're right. We never thought of that. You're free to go. Have a nice evening."

I was right. The bluff didn't work.

The one in front hit me in the solar plexus. I bent over and almost puked. The one in back yanked me upright and held me in place for more punishment. The guy in front caught me with a haymaker across the cheekbone. Things began to go dim. He hit me in the face several more times, but it didn't hurt anymore.

Three or four rib shots from the front, and the guy in back let go. I slumped to the ground. The parts of me that still had feeling hurt like a son-of-a-bitch. They kicked me in the ribs and head. Then several heavy hits in the arms and legs. There was pain at first with each blow, then numbness, then they walked away, their footsteps echoing down the alley.

"We'll be back if you insist," one of them called back to me. "You fuck with the Captain again, next time we finish it."

I tried to yell back to remember to tell Jeremy what I said, but my speaking mechanism was out of order.

As was almost everything else. I could barely move. And I couldn't see. My eyes were swelling shut, and blood flowed out from everywhere. I lay there in dirt and grease from the road mixed with my blood into a sickening paste, caked all over my face and in my hair.

And I had just had my trench coat cleaned.

I could lie there all night without being found. People rarely used this alley. Or worse, winos and junkies would find me and steal my wallet and trench coat. And maybe my shoes. They'd probably leave the Mickey Mouse watch.

I felt in my pocket for my cell phone. Just bending my shoulder and elbow shot an excruciating pain up my arm. I thought I would pass out. Maybe I did a couple times.

After a few tries I was able to get the phone out. I held it with one hand and speed dialed the office with my thumb. The other arm and hand wouldn't move and had no feeling. I had to do it by feel. Both eyes were closed. Willa answered.

"Willa," I squeaked. I could barely make a sound. "It's Stan. I'm out here in the alley. Call nine-one-one."

"Stan? In the alley? What happened?"

Then everything went dark.

Chapter 12

When I woke up, I was on a hospital gurney somewhere in a hallway. People in hospital uniforms bustled up and down the hallway, ignoring me. I could feel the bandages on my face and around my torso. One of my arms was wrapped and suspended by a cable from an overhead steel frame. One leg was similarly elevated. One eye was closed, the other one barely open. It seemed like one of everything was broken. I hoped my balls had made it through the meltdown. At least one, anyway.

I ran my tongue around inside my mouth feeling for missing teeth. A couple of them were loose, but they were all there. At least the ones I had before the fight started.

An IV was dripping something into my arm through a tube. Everything hurt. I passed out again.

When I came to, I was in a hospital room. Willa was sitting in a chair at the end of my bed reading a book. Amanda was in another chair pulled up close to the bed. I scanned the room with my good eye, which could hardly see anything. A shadow of a man stood with his back to me looking out the window into what I assumed was a parking lot.

Amanda said, "He's awake."

I tried to speak, but my lips were swollen from the beating. I tried to say, "Who's minding the store?" It came out like, "Whosh ninig da shore?"

Willa said, "Rodney's manning the phone. Not much store to mind without you there."

"Oh, great," I mumbled. "Rodney."

"Yeah, he's taken over your office. Maybe he can book some more work for us."

She laughed. I groaned. Then she said, "Your only client sent his man here."

The shadow turned around. It was Sanford.

"What the fuck happened, Bentworth?" Sandford said.

"Don't say 'fuck' in front of the ladies," I said through the bandages in my new Rocky Balboa tenth round dialect.

"Mr. Overbee wants to know. Does this have anything to do with the case?"

"No. Family fight."

"What were you doing working on something else? Mr. Overbee has you on full retainer."

"Like I said. It was a family matter. Off the clock."

That seemed to satisfy him. "Mr. Overbee wants to help," he said. "Who did it?"

"Two Army guys. Don't know them. Amanda's boyfriend set them on me."

"Stanley," Amanda said, "Captain Pugh is not my boyfriend."

"He doesn't know that. Anybody got a mirror?" I wanted to see how bad it was.

"No mirrors," Willa said. "We can't stand looking at you, so you sure couldn't. No point in you being more miserable and depressed."

"I look that bad?"

"No. It's an improvement," she said.

"What's happening with Buford?" I asked Sanford.

"At home. Ankle bracelet. House arrest."

"You still his lawyer?"

"No. Just his driver. He said you told him he needed a better-looking lawyer."

"Sorry."

"That's okay. He needs a better-looking detective now."

Turnabout is fair play.

"Tell Buford I'll see him when I'm discharged. How long have I been here?"

"Three days," Willa said. "The doctor said once you woke up you'd be able to go home soon if there's somebody there to look after you for a while."

"My house," Amanda said. "I'll look after him."

Oh great, I thought.

"And when you're at work," Willa said to Amanda, "I can move the office into your house if that's okay."

Just then the doctor came in. He brought my chart with him and sat on the edge of my bed.

"Mr. Bentworth, I'm Dr. Goldenberg. You came through this pretty good." He looked at the chart. "A dislocated shoulder, which we reset. A thin fracture in your shin. Another on your arm. You'll need casts for a few weeks."

He pulled my nightgown up and pressed on my belly.

"No internal injuries, although I don't know how. A couple of fractured ribs and some facial bone fractures, all of which should heal up okay. Watch those loose teeth. They should set themselves. You might have a bit of a bent nose too."

"Might help with my undercover Mafia work." Now for the part that had me worried. "How about my eyes?"

"They should be okay. We'll know better when we take the bandages off, probably tomorrow. You'll have a couple of shiners."

"Will I be able to play the violin again?"

The Doctor shook his head. "You know how many times I've heard that joke?"

"Yeah, but I never had the opportunity to tell it before."

"What did you do to piss those guys off, Mr. Bentworth? Tell them a joke?"

Now that made me laugh. It hurt so much that I stopped.

"When you go home," the Doc said, "You're going to need some equipment and physical therapy. Are you up for that?"

He stood up and looked down at me.

"Can't afford it," I said. "Hell, I don't know how I'm going to pay for this."

"No insurance?"

"None."

"Well, at least get some crutches and maybe a wheel chair."

Amanda spoke up. "Stanley, I've still got Daddy's crutches from when he fell off the stoop. They're old, but they might still work."

Our father had been accident-prone. Particularly when he was drunk, which was most of the time. They say I'm a chip off the old block.

I said, "You got to get me out of here, Doc. Have you seen what a hospital costs these days? Almost as expensive as gas and cigarettes. And lap dances."

Speaking of which—expenses, not lap dances—as the doc left, the lady from administration was there with forms about how I could pay for everything.

"Send the bill to the Army," I said.

That afternoon, after all my company had left, Bill Penrod came to see me.

"Willa called. What the hell happened to you?" he said.

"You ought to see the other guy."

He pulled up a chair.

"Does this have something to do with the Overbee case?"

"No. This is a different fight."

"Want to tell me about it?"

I explained the circumstances about Captain Jeremy Pugh and the Bobbsey twins. He sat without comment until I finished the story.

"Get a good look at them?" he asked.

"Good enough. They were just messengers, though."

"If you can identify them and testify, I'll have them picked up on assault and battery."

He started to light a cigarette and then caught himself and put it back in the pack.

"They've probably disappeared into some deep, dark military intelligence safe house," I said. "Besides, they were just following orders. The Nuremburg syndrome. Captain Pugh is running the show."

"Anything I can do about him?"

"Other than lean on him, I don't think there's much you can do. Nothing concrete to tie him to the two goons other than my word against his."

I rolled on my side just to change where the pressure was. It didn't help.

"Sounds like you want to handle this yourself."

"I want to keep the guy away from my sister. Whether I exact revenge for this beat-down will depend on circumstances. I'm not equipped to take on Army Intelligence."

Bill grinned and looked away.

"Maybe we could write him a citation for a busted headlight."

"Yeah, right, Bill. That'd sure even things out."

"Seriously, Stan, our black and whites can harass the shit out of this moke. And make sure he knows why. We've done it before."

He was right. Bill and I had done it more than once back in the day.

"God, that seems like such a long time ago," I said.

"And only yesterday too. You want me to do it?"

"Not yet. I'll let you know." I was thinking about how Buford had disapproved when I said I let the cops clean up my messes. I'd handle this mess myself.

Chapter 13

The next morning my cell phone rang and woke me up. I looked at the caller I.D. Buford was calling. I pushed the button to raise the bed and answered.

"How are you, Stan?"

"Been better."

"Sanford said you look pretty bad. Was this beat-down related to you working for me?"

Everybody asked that.

"No."

"You working for somebody else?"

They ask that too.

"No. This was a private matter."

"That's what Sanford said. Who are the two Army guys that beat you up?"

"I don't know them."

"Who's the guy that set them on you?"

"Army Intelligence officer. Captain Jeremy Pugh." I found it difficult to say his name without spitting.

"You want help?" Buford asked. I could imagine the kind of help he would send.

"No, I'll take care of it."

"Like you took care of it this time?"

"I'll be ready for them next time."

"Careful. You might wind up my cellmate."

"I think I can make a case for self-defense given what they already did to me."

"You probably can. I guess you didn't make any headway on my case."

"Not yet. I hope to get back to work soon."

I meant that. I wanted to work. This lying around in a bed was getting to be a pain. And I already had more than enough pain.

"I hope you do too," Buford said. "I need you out there solving the murder. This hanging around the house with Melissa and Serena gets old fast."

"I'll trade places. I'd never get tired of looking at Serena."

"It ain't all it's cracked up to be."

"You always have Sanford and son."

"Who?"

"Sanford and Ramon."

"Oh, yeah. I forgot. We can play cribbage."

"Sure." I turned onto my other side and adjusted the pillow. "How's business?"

"I lost a few clients because of this shit. And my picture made the papers. I had to beef up security. I figure on being visited soon. The mob."

"Well, we tried." I didn't have a solution for that one.

"That shit'll never go away. Those bastards are relentless. I might have to sell everything, cash in, and leave the country. After I beat this murder rap and get this fucking ankle bracelet off. The son-of-a-bitch chafes my skin."

"How did you manage to draw house arrest?" I asked. "They don't usually do that for violent crimes."

"I am the mayor's silent financial advisor, Stan. The judge's too. They both want me out here working."

"Penrod must have pitched a bitch."

"The police commissioner told him to back off."

"Him too?"

"Him too."

"Next time I get a parking ticket," I said, "I'll bring it to you."

Chapter 14

Doc Goldenberg discharged me about three days later. The bandages were off my eyes, and, except for some residual swelling around the lids, I could see okay. I still had bandages on my head, stitches in my face, and casts on my arm and leg.

On my way from the bed to the pink lady's wheelchair, I took a look in the mirror. I looked like the goalee in a javelin contest. Victor Frankenstein would have been proud.

Amanda drove me to her house. I wanted to go to my apartment, but she wouldn't have it. She was enjoying the caregiver role. I was not enjoying the caretaker role.

She set me up in Rodney's room.

"You'll sleep here," she said. "He can sleep on the couch." The room was an experience. Vampire and punk rock posters, lava lamps, a desk loaded with computer equipment, shelves of stereo gear, and laundry and junk everywhere.

"It's like living on the set of The Rocky Horror Picture Show," I said.

"You want him to clean it?"

"No. I don't want to know what might be living under all this grunge."

Amanda dug out Dad's old crutches, and I was able to get around with them, but I wouldn't be able to drive. The casts on my leg and arm would get in the way, and besides, the drugs were too good.

"Don't worry, Stanley, Rodney can take you wherever you want to go," Amanda said.

"Terrific. Where is he now?"

"He goes into the office every day. He's talking about becoming a full partner in the detective agency."

"Fat chance. When do I get to go back to work?"

"When you're better. Rodney will drive you."

"I don't think I want to ride in that heap of his," I said. "Besides, there isn't room for me with all the trash he has in there."

"He's been driving your car. Says it looks more professional."

"Oh, great. With his pants down around his knees, I hope he doesn't leave any wedgies on the upholstery."

"Wait 'til you see him," she said.

I got to see Rodney that evening when he came home. I barely recognized him. He was wearing a white shirt, suit and tie, and a new trench coat. His hair was cut, combed, and back to its natural color. He had shaved. I had forgotten what a good-looking young man Rodney could be.

"What the hell happened to you?" I asked.

"Hi, Uncle Stanley. I remembered what you said about cleaning up to work with clients. This is the new me. I kind of like it."

"What will your friends say? The ones who still recognize you."

"Friends? Maybe you never noticed, but I don't have friends."

"Maybe you will now. What's this about clients? You have clients?"

"Not yet. I've been waiting for you to get back. Mom said I'm to be your chauffer now until the casts come off. You want to go anywhere?"

Amanda called from the kitchen, "Not yet, Rodney. Uncle Stanley isn't ready to go anywhere just yet, dear."

Each day I got better. I still needed the crutches and couldn't drive, but I was getting around the little house on my own. Willa came by each morning. The pretense was that we could keep the business going, which involved answering the office phone, which she had redirected to her cell, and putting off all potential clients until I got better. Rodney did the same thing at the office for walk-ins. That was the pretense. The real reason she was there was to look after me so Amanda could go to work. She left each evening when Amanda got home.

I have to say I was eating better. Those ladies could cook.

When I was able I tried to help out around the house, washing dishes and doing laundry with my crutches holding me up as I leaned on the sink or clothes washer. Those tasks didn't often last long, though. I'd tire after a few minutes and have to go lie on the couch for a while.

One evening I was sitting in the living room trying to make my way through the latest cop TV show. How come those guys are always young hunks that get to work with gorgeous babes? I'm a middle aged hump, and all I get to work with is Willa. The best-looking woman I know is my sister. Life ain't fair.

Rodney was standing at the window looking out and probably wishing he could drive me somewhere.

He said, "Uncle Stanley. Guess who's here. The Captain."

Damn. I hadn't asked Rodney to bring Roscoe home from the office, mainly because I didn't want him to know where I kept it stashed. And he'd have needed the combination to the safe. Not a good idea.

Then I remembered the shotgun.

"Get me Grandpa's shotgun from the closet."

Rodney got the shotgun, and I stood with my crutches propped under my arms and opened the breech. The shotgun was loaded. I closed the breech and got up against the wall beside the door. The doorbell rang.

"Open it," I whispered to Rodney.

He opened the door. Jeremy said from the stoop, "Who the hell are you?"

"I'm Rodney. Go away."

He started to close the door. Jeremy pushed it open again.

"I didn't recognize you in drag. Get your mother, kid. I want to talk to her."

"She doesn't want to talk to you," Rodney said.

"Get her anyway. Or I will."

"Who is it, Rodney?" Amanda called from the kitchen.

"It's your asshole ex-boyfriend," Rodney answered.

"You little shit," Jeremy said. He was still on the stoop out of my sight.

"Step back," I whispered to Rodney.

Rodney stepped back and Jeremy began to come through the door, his eyes on Rodney. I swung the shotgun with full force and hit him across the bridge of his nose with the barrel. *Thump!* Must have been a bit of a surprise. He fell back out of sight. I hobbled into the doorway. He was sprawled on the sidewalk just beyond the stoop, holding his face with both hands, blood streaming out of his nose and down his chin. I pointed the shotgun directly at him.

"You have a short memory, Captain. I told you to leave my sister alone."

He rolled over and got up on his hands and knees. A shiner was forming around both eyes. Not as pretty as mine, but he'd have it for a while as a reminder. He pulled out a handkerchief and wiped his face.

"Now get the fuck out of here," I said. "The next time you come back, me and this shotgun will decorate the sidewalk with your insides. At the first sign of you, I shoot. No questions asked. No explanations offered. None accepted. Just a big bang. Leave. Now. While you still can."

I looked out at his car. The windows and headlight had been replaced, but the dent was still in the door.

"You don't learn too easy yourself, Bentworth. Do you need another session with my boys?"

"Thanks, stupid. My sister and nephew just heard you confess to putting them onto me. That might come in handy when I take your ass to court. Oh, by the way. Did I say leave?"

I pulled the hammers back on the old shotgun. I wondered whether it would even fire. Maybe blow up in my face.

He stood up and backed slowly towards his car, keeping an eye on me and the shotgun. About that time a police cruiser pulled up.

"I called them, Stanley." Amanda was standing behind me now.

"I can handle this, Mandy."

"You're not a hundred percent yet. A little help can't hurt."

"I think Uncle Stanley did just fine, Mom." He seemed proud of the old man.

Two uniforms got out of the cruiser.

"Wait right there," one of them said to Jeremy.

He stood with Jeremy and the car while the other uniform came to the door.

"Everything under control, Detective, I mean, Mr. Bentworth?"

"Everything's fine," I said. "Thanks for stopping by."

"Sergent Penrod spread the word at the precinct. When the call came in, we knew it was you. Anything we can do to help, we will."

He walked back to Jeremy's car.

"Looks like we have a couple of violations here, Fred," he said to his partner.

He took his nightstick off his belt, went in front of the Beamer, and busted a headlight and parking light lens. Then he took out his citation pad, wrote on it, tore off the page, and handed it to Jeremy, who wisely accepted it and kept his mouth shut.

"Get away from these people's house and do not bother them again," the other uniform said to Jeremy. "Otherwise, you'd be surprised at how many of your days can be ruined."

Everyone drove away. But I was more than certain that I hadn't seen the last of Captain Jeremy Pugh.

My cell phone rang, and I horsed it out of my pocket. Buford again.

"How's everything going? You back to work yet?"

"Not yet, but soon, maybe tomorrow. I'll call you from the office and we can get together."

"Any more problems with that Army guy?"

"Funny you should ask."

I told him about what had just gone down.

"Sounds like you and the cops have a handle on it."

"Yeah, but I don't think I've heard the last of him."

"Why's that?"

"He made it clear. I'll probably get another visit from the two goons."

Chapter 15

By the next day I was suffering from terminal cabin fever after doing nothing but sitting in the living room watching daytime TV. If ever there was a reason for a man not to retire, Jerry Springer and Law and Order reruns are it.

Amanda had taken the day off so Willa could do some work at the office. After a session of me pleading and her objecting, I wore her down and persuaded her to take me to the office. She dropped me off at the front door.

"Will you be able to get up the stairs okay?" she asked.

"Sure. See you later."

The stairs were not easy. It took me a half hour to climb the two flights. When I went in the office, Willa was busy at her desk writing checks to pay bills.

"What are you doing here?" she asked and went back to writing in the check book.

"Got bored at the Amanda Bentworth boarding house and nursing home," I said. "What are you doing?"

"Paying bills." This time she didn't look up. All business, that lady.

"Didn't you pay bills a couple weeks ago?"

"Funny thing about bills. You pay them and they just come back. Like mowing the lawn or feeding your cat."

"I don't mow the lawn, and I don't have a cat," I said.

"You don't pay bills, either. It's a wonder we're not both in debtor's prison."

"Both? I'm the one not paying bills."

She shook her head. "One of which is my salary. I've been warding off the old bill collector myself."

I did my best to put on a guilty face, but it didn't work.

"I'll be at Amanda's tomorrow to look after you," she said.

"I don't like all this attention. Amanda and you hovering over me, bringing me coffee and food, doing my meds, fluffing my pillow."

"Don't get used to it."

I went in the office. There sat Rodney at a second desk.

"Where did the desk come from?"

"Salvation Army thrift shop. I paid ten bucks for it. They threw the chair in. Getting it up the stairs was the hard part."

"Tell me about it."

I sat at my desk and dialed Buford's number.

"Buford, I'm back in the office. Anything happening with your case?"

I lit my last cigarette ever and tossed the match on the floor. Just because I could.

"Got a continuance," Buford said. "Maybe two months before I go to trial. I want this thing cleared up by then."

"I'm working on it. How about if I come see you this afternoon? We'll kick it around."

"That would be good. This place is shut down like Fort Knox. I'll tell the guards to let you through. You still driving that piece of shit station wagon?"

"Yeah. Rodney's my driver now."

"I guess you heard. That Captain Pugh won't be bothering your sister any more."

That was a surprise. A nice surprise. I couldn't wait to hear why.

"No, I didn't hear anything. What happened?"

"In this morning's paper. Had an accident in his boat. Must have been a leaky fuel line and a short circuit. The boat blew up in the middle of the river."

"Was he on board?" That would be too good to be true.

"They think so. Somebody had to have sailed it out there. They didn't find a body. But then, they didn't find much else either. He's on the menu. The fish got him."

I didn't trust the good news. "Could be maybe it wasn't an accident?" I said.

"Couldn't say. But I bet that Penrod murder cop comes to see you about it."

"He will. I have an alibi. I was imprisoned at my sister's house. And can't get around on my own. Shit, I can barely make it to the john without help."

"Yeah. Convenient, ain't it? Alibi-wise, that is."

We hung up, and I told Rodney, "We're going out this afternoon. But I want to get some lunch first. You can help me down the stairs."

"You want me to go for carryout?"

"No thanks. And don't you start mothering me too," I said as we went past Willa's desk. "Leave that to your mom. And Grandma Willa here."

Willa made an audible snort and slammed the checkbook closed.

We left the office and went to the stairway. Rodney supported me with my good arm around his shoulder and his arm around my waist. He held the crutches in his other hand. We hobbled along like conjoined twins and went down the stairs. It took about ten minutes.

We went out the front door, and I looked up and down the street. About a block away was an olive drab Chevy parked on the street.

"Stay with me across the street," I told Rodney, but I didn't tell him why. I didn't think the Army guys would do anything in front of a witness.

But I was sure they were pissed about their beloved Captain getting hit broadside in the face with a shotgun barrel. Not to mention being blown up.

Rodney walked with me across the street and into Ray's.

"You want lunch?" I asked.

"No. I had my usual," he said. He turned and headed back across the street.

Some things never change.

I went in and slowly lowered myself into a booth. The lunch crowd had left, so I had the joint to myself. I leaned my crutches against the wall and looked at the menu. Not that I had to, but it gave me something to do.

Bunny came out of the kitchen and stared at me. It took her a while to figure out who I was. She scribbled an order for me, passed it through to the kitchen, and came over to where I was sitting. She looked at me a while before speaking. She had tears in her eyes. Great. Another woman getting all weepy over a few cuts and bruises.

"Stan, what happened?"

"Fell off my skateboard."

"Were you in the hospital?"

"Yeah. Maybe a week. How do I look?"

"Not good, but better than when you had the hangover."

I could always count on Bunny to lighten a dark moment.

"Nobody told me you got hurt," she said. "I wondered why I hadn't seen you. I'd have come to visit you. You got some place to stay?"

"Yeah, don't worry."

I finished breakfast. Bill Penrod came in and sat across from me.

"Willa said you were here. She was right. You do look like shit. Who's that guy working for you?"

"That's Rodney. You remember him."

"Holy shit! The punker? What a difference! How'd you get him to scrub up?"

"His idea. Wants to be a private dick like me."

"Man, the way you look now, nobody'd want to follow in your footsteps."

"What's up, Bill?" As if I didn't know.

"You hear about the boat that blew up in the river? The boat owned by Captain Jeremy Pugh? The boat upon which said Jeremy Pugh probably died?"

"Yeah. Real shame, isn't it. I'm all broke up about it. I've heard that was a nice boat."

"You have anything to do with it?"

Of course, he had to ask. Just doing his job.

"Me? Look at me. What could I do? Besides, all my time is accounted for."

"Maybe, maybe not. The charge could have been set at any time. Could have been detonated from a cell phone. From a sick bed, even."

On the one hand I was proud that Bill credited me with having the savvy and balls to blow up a boat. On the other hand, I was uncomfortable being a suspect.

"You know me," I said. "I don't know shit about explosives. Did you find a detonator?"

"Christ, Stan, we didn't even find the rudder. That was one hell of a blast. Should have kicked off a tsunami and wiped out the whole fucking town. There wasn't anything left of the boat."

"And no body."

"Right. He hasn't been seen since it happened. His wife is worried sick."

"She say anything to you about leaving him?"

"No. Why?"

"That's what he told Amanda when she threatened to call her."

"He say why?"

"No. But I'd guess based on how he treated Amanda, that he was knocking his wife around too. Might be some motive there."

"Interesting theory. But she seemed worried about him."

"Yeah. No body. Insurance companies make you wait seven years. That'd make anybody worry."

"In the meantime, you are still a person of interest."

I didn't like him saying it that way. How many times had the two of us said the same thing to a suspect just to rattle him?

"Who besides you knows I was having trouble with the guy?" I asked.

"Well, the whole fucking precinct for starters. And whoever your sister told at work. Probably the whole town."

"So there's no chance of you burying it."

"No chance."

"Those Army guys think I did it."

"How do you know?"

"They're following me around again. They got no boss telling them to do it now, but there they are. Look down the street when you leave. Olive drab Chevy."

After Bill left, I finished breakfast and called Rodney to come get me. He was there in about a minute, and we walked across the street. The olive drab Chevy was still there. The glint of the afternoon sun reflected off of binocular lenses through the windshield in the passenger's side. Or maybe a camera lens. Or a telescopic lens.

"Watch for red laser lights," I told Rodney.

"Huh?" he said.

As we crossed the street, a black and white pulled up next to the Army car. The cops rolled down their window and talked to the soldiers, after which the Army car pulled out and sped away. Good old Bill. Doing what he could.

Rodney and I went around the building to my car, which Rodney had parked in the alley. He helped me in, and I gave him directions to Buford's house.

Chapter 16

This time Officer Bob waved us right into the compound, but security was tight at Buford's. A guard in a black suit and sunglasses was stationed at Buford's personal gatehouse. He checked our identification and waved us through. Two black SUVs stood in the driveway near the entrance. Another black suit stood at the doorway talking on a walkie-talkie.

Rodney helped me out of the car and to the door.

"Wait in the car, please," I said. He got a disappointed look on his face, which I pretended not to notice.

The black suit stood aside and let me in. He said that Mr. Overbee was waiting on the patio.

I went through the house and out to the patio. Buford was on a chaise lounge with Missy on one side and Serena on the other.

Buford got up and said, "Let's go in the study where we won't bore the ladies with business."

However this conversation was going to go, he didn't want anyone else in on it. Neither did I. Especially Missy and Serena.

We went into the study and sat in facing leather easy chairs. Gravity allowed me to sink into the chair, but I'd need help getting up. I laid my crutches on the floor beside the chair.

Ramon was there right away with drinks for both of us. We waited for him to leave.

"You look like shit," Buford said.

"I get that a lot."

"Any trouble getting in?"

"No. Bob and the Men In Black passed me right through."

"Some of Sanford's guys. I brought them on after I was outed."

"Tell me about the boat bombing."

"You mean the boat accident?" he asked, looking away.

"Come on. You might get an onboard fire from a spark and gas leak, but they said there wasn't anything left of that boat but flotsam."

He took a sip. I took a healthy swallow.

"My boys had nothing to do with it, if that's what you're thinking," he said. "Did you read about him being Army Intelligence and Homeland Security looking into it?"

"Think they'll find anything?"

"Not if whoever did it is competent. I understand some of those terrorists are real good with explosives."

"Well, his soldier pals think I had something to do with it. They've been stalking me."

"I'll tell Sanford. He might be able to discourage them."

"Okay, but don't go blowing up any Army vehicles. At least not in front of my office. I don't have the alibi any more."

He didn't answer. I had the distinct impression that Buford Overbee would be a good friend to have and a fearsome enemy. I changed the subject.

"Let's talk about your case. Did the cops tell you where they found the gun?"

"In the trunk of my Rolls. Under the wheel in the spare tire compartment. Whoever offed Vitole must have planted it there."

That didn't leave many probable suspects.

"Who has access to your car?"

"Me and Sanford."

"Anyone else have keys?"

"Not that I know of."

We were getting closer.

"Do you think Sanford bumped Vitole?"

Buford stopped. Then he said, "He knew we were having trouble. He knew that Vitole could put me out of business. Sanford could have done it and with good reason. Without me he'd have nothing."

Sanford was getting to be a sure thing.

"Do you want me to work that angle?"

"I want you to work any angle that gets this ankle bracelet off and these charges dropped. I don't care if the Pope did it."

It surprised me at first that Buford would so readily throw his old friend under the bus. But then, he had a history of doing just that when his own hide was at stake.

"Did the cops question Sanford?"

"Not much. He has an alibi."

"Didn't he drive you to Vitole's house when you went to see him? Is that his alibi?"

"No. I didn't want anyone else implicated. Didn't know what might happen. I was packing. I drove myself."

"What's Sanford's alibi?"

"Ramon. They were here shooting pool in the rec room all day."

"So, they're each other's alibi. What are their full names?"

"Ramon Sanchez. Probably not his real name. He's your garden variety undocumented alien. Smartest kid I ever met. The only guy I know can beat me at chess."

"And Sanford?"

"It's the only name I've ever known him by."

He put down his drink and looked at me. "I don't think it was either one of them, Stan, although they're both loyal employees."

"You have a theory?" Sometimes—oftentimes—your best leads come from the people who hire you.

"My guess is that Vitole was shaking down other guys. One of them probably got to him like we did, only whoever it was took extreme measures to get him off their back. People in witness protection are not usually Sunday School teachers."

"How could they have planted the gun?"

"Any time I was out somewhere. Or when I was in the holding cell. Get the trunk open, plant the piece, don't leave prints, don't get caught."

"Was the Rolls out of here during your incarceration?"

"Sure. Selena and Melissa have Sanford or Ramon take them shopping or wherever."

"How could the killer have gotten the gun in the first place?"

"That I don't know."

"Do you know whether it's actually yours?"

"Could be. They haven't shown it to me. Nothing's missing from the collection."

"Are all the guns in these display cases?"

"Stan, you can't open a drawer or box in this house without finding a loaded piece. I'm paranoid about being caught unaware and unarmed. Look down at the side of the chair you're sitting in."

I looked down. The leather chair had a leather holster stitched onto its side. The brown grips of a .32 automatic pistol stuck up out of the holster.

"Do you have many guests?"

"I sometimes receive clients here. Ones who already know what I look like."

"And who know who you used to be? Could one of your clients be in the same boat you are? Getting shaken down by Vitole?"

"I suppose anything's possible."

"Could someone like that have taken one of your pieces?"

"Might have."

"And planted it in your car?"

"That's far-fetched."

"We'll play hell getting the feds to release a list of witness protection clients," I said.

"Penrod said the same thing when I suggested he look into it. No, the cops are content to have me. They don't need anyone else. Case closed. Job well done. You used to be in that business, Stan. Isn't that how it works?"

"That's how it works. Can you get me a list of your clients? You can leave out the movie stars and other famous people. Just the ones with vague backgrounds."

"That won't be a long list. I'll get it together and send it to you."

"Was Vitole's wife there when you visited?"

"No. He said he was alone."

"That's what he said when I visited. I guess she works. Too bad. She could have told the cops he was alive when you left."

It was time to get into the difficult parts of the case.

"Now," I said. "We agreed that I should chase down any lead, any hunch, whatever."

"Yes."

"What about the ladies in your life? Missy and Serena?"

Buford paused. "I never gave that the first thought."

"I did. Do I chase it?"

"Chase it," he said, taking another sip of his drink.

"Even Missy?"

"Especially Missy. She's very protective and has the balls and brains to do something like that. Serena is dumber than a bag of ball peen hammers and doesn't think about anything past her hairdo, nails, and makeup."

"And what do I do if it starts to look like Missy?"

He stopped and thought about it. "You tell me," he said. "I handle it from there."

I started thinking about opportunity, who had it, who was likely to use it.

"While you were out that morning, did the others have a way to get over to Vitole's house?"

"Yeah. There are several SUVs here. And both the girls have their own cars."

"Were they here when you got back?"

"Don't remember."

"Were Sanford and Ramon?"

"Don't remember."

That brought our meeting to a close. I finished my drink and started to struggle to get up from the easy chair, Ramon was there in a flash helping me up.

"Does he hear everything we say?" I asked Buford.

"I do not listen, Señor. I only watch."

I hoped he was telling the truth. I wasn't ready for him and Sanford to know they were suspects.

Chapter 17

I lay in the bed on my back, still in pain. Almost everything hurt. I got a cigarette from the pack on the nightstand and fumbled with the book of matches tucked under the cellophane. Nothing is easy when only one hand works. Bunny sat up next to me, took the pack, extracted the matches, and lit my last cigarette ever.

Rodney had dropped me off at Ray's the day before, and I wound up here at Bunny's. I'm not sure how that happened, but I was glad.

"It's good to be back," I said.

"It's better when you can move," she said. She got up to get me an ashtray.

"You always wanted to be on top anyway."

She handed me the ashtray. I put it on the bed next to me, and she stretched out again.

"I thought you quit smoking," she said.

"Tomorrow."

She pulled the sheet up over herself.

"You don't want me looking at you?" I said.

"You've seen better. You married better."

That hit a sore spot. "Don't remind me. Besides, what's wrong with your looks?"

"Stretch marks. Cellulite."

"They're nothing compared to my scars."

"On a guy they look tough. On us we just look old."

"Tough?"

"Well, not yet. They have to heal and scar up. Right now you look like you've been in a chainsaw fight."

"But I'll look tough? Hell, I'd have paid money for that."

"Wait'll you get the hospital bill."

We lay quiet for a while, looking at the ceiling while I smoked my cigarette.

"You want to talk about us?" she said.

"About us? We're here now. What's to talk about?"

"Tomorrow."

"I always left that up to you."

She rolled over on her side and faced me.

"Maybe that was the problem, Stan. Maybe you shouldn't have."

"You've got a point. It never turned out good when you were in charge of tomorrow."

"Give me another chance?"

"Don't I always?"

"You do."

"And then next thing I know you're gone again."

"That's happened."

"Why would this time be any different?"

"It could be," she said. "Maybe it will be."

"You making a promise?"

"No," she said. She got out of the bed. "I got to get to work."

"Me too. Help me get my clothes on?"

"Why not? I helped you get them off. Do you want to take a shower?"

"Not with all these bandages. I'll get a sponge bath later at home."

"You want one now?" she said.

"Thanks, but I really have to get to work. A sponge bath would take a long time."

"I'd hope so."

We got dressed with Bunny dressing both of us. Damn, I felt useless. I was able to get to her car without help. She lived on the first floor. She took me to Ray's for breakfast.

Afterwards I called Rodney to come escort me to the office and help me up the stairs. He was there in a heartbeat. Always eager to please.

"You remember Rodney," I said to Bunny.

"Oh, yeah. The nephew. I liked the other shirt better, Rodney, but the shave and haircut is an improvement."

We walked across the street. The olive drab Chevy was there again. They were still watching. I considered calling Bill Penrod, but by the time we got up the stairs I had forgotten about it.

"Good morning, Willa."

"Good morning. Amanda called. Just checking up. I didn't know where you were, so she was worried. Rodney said he left you with Bunny, so I figured you were okay."

"Did either of you think to call my cell phone?"

"I didn't want to get you out of the middle of somebody."

Man, that Willa had a mouth on her.

"Rodney," I said, "can you get us one of those whiteboards with felt-tip markers? We're going to need one for talking points for this case. The office supply store should have them."

"Yeah, I can get one. Am I helping you with the case?"

"Yes. I'd like to bounce some of my ideas off you, and I need the board to organize them."

"Man, that's cool. Can I get a badge like yours?"

"Sure. Google 'private investigator badge' and you'll find them. Mine cost about thirty bucks."

"I'll do it when I get back," he said. "Do I have to pay for it myself?"

"You do."

"What about a gun?"

"No gun."

"Why not?"

Kids always whine and ask why not whenever you tell them they can't have or do something. Usually, "because I say so" is a sufficient answer, but in this case I had the law on my side.

"Because you have to be twenty-one to get a carry permit, is why not. Now go get the whiteboard."

Willa gave Rodney some money from petty cash, and he headed out.

I went into my office and got Roscoe out of the safe. It hadn't been cleaned in a long time. I took it out of the holster and unloaded it. My gun cleaning kit was in a desk drawer under a bunch of other junk. I got it out and carefully cleaned the piece, enjoying the procedure and the unmistakable scent of gun oil.

I wasn't going to go anywhere without Roscoe now that the ever-diligent soldier boys were on my trail again. My badge was still pinned to the holster. I reloaded the gun, put it in the holster, and put the assembly into my top desk drawer.

I called Ray's Diner. Bunny answered.

"What's for lunch?" I asked.

"How about a taco?"

After the laughter faded, I said, "Can't make it over there today. My orderly is out on an errand and won't be back."

"Shall I bring you something?"

"Yeah. Bring something for Willa too."

In about a half hour, Bunny was there with three club sandwiches in Styrofoam boxes. Willa was pleased that she wouldn't have to go out and that we'd thought of her. I let her think it was Bunny's idea.

The three of us ate together. Willa kept looking at Bunny with a suspicious eye. Willa did not hide her disapproval. Bunny would break my heart again. It had occurred to me too.

Rodney was back after lunch with a big flat carton. He took it into my office and took the whiteboard out of the box.

"Hang it over there," I said pointing to the blank wall opposite the window.

He went to his truck and came back with his toolbox. In a matter of minutes the board was hanging on the wall. Accessories included a pack of markers, an eraser, and a spray bottle of cleaner. We were ready to go.

I told Rodney to stand at the board and make a chart of suspects' names with columns alongside for means, motive, opportunity, alibi, and the date I interviewed each suspect. I called out names, and he wrote them on the board. Mr. and Mrs. Sproles, Vitole's wife, Missy, Serena, Sanford, and Ramon.

On another part of the board I had him list witnesses along with the date interviewed and comments about what they saw or knew. So far the witness list was empty.

Rodney had nice block-letter handwriting. I was surprised.

"You know, Uncle Stanley, we could have done all this with a spreadsheet on the computer."

"Yeah, but then I couldn't lean back in my chair and ponder them. Call me old-fashioned. This is how we used to do it when I worked homicide."

Across the top of the board we made a timeline that traced events related to the case by date and time. We'd add to the timeline as we learned new things.

"How about this?" Rodney said. "Every time we update the board, I'll take a picture of it and upload it to the computer? That way, we'll have a record."

"Okay. And print one for Willa to put in the file."

Willa came in to look at our artwork.

"The Y people," she said.

"What?" I said.

"Almost everybody's name ends with a Y. Stanley, Rodney, Missy, Bunny, Jeremy, Mandy, Vitole.

"Mandy, Bunny, and Jeremy aren't part of this case," I said.

"But they fit the pattern."

"Vitole doesn't end in a Y.

"It sounds like it does. So does Overbee."

"You left out Mickey," I said.

"Who's Mickey?" she asked.

I tapped my watch. She laughed and went back to her office.

Rodney and I spent the afternoon kicking around theories and opinions about various aspects of the case. Rodney's contributions were superficial at best, but I needed someone to bounce off whatever crazy notion I had. Penrod and I used to do that a lot, and I missed that part of being a murder cop.

Chapter 18

When we ran out of ideas, Rodney and I called it a day. He helped me down the stairs. The effort wore me out, but I was getting better at doing it without help. He had to grab me to keep me from falling only every two or three stairs now. We went out the back door into the alley. It was dark, the only light coming from a naked bulb on the building across the alley.

"I'll wait here while you get the car." I told him.

The car was parked a couple blocks away. Rodney went running down the alley.

I didn't see them coming. My vision still wasn't what it ought to be and my reflexes not as quick. As near as I can figure, they were hiding in the next doorway up, a recessed alcove that opened into a suite of unoccupied offices. My back was to that doorway. Next thing I knew, the same two Army thugs were in front of me.

I tried to get Roscoe out of the holster, but the stupid badge got in the way and kept me from unsnapping the trigger guard strap. One of the goons grabbed my good arm and the other one yanked the holster off my belt and threw the gun, holster, and badge across the alley.

As before, one of them pinned me from behind in a full nelson, and the other one stood in front of me. My only hope was that Rodney would see what was going on and speed towards them to make them release me so I could hit them with a crutch or whatever. I know, not much of a plan, but what else could I do?

"This time we'll finish it," one of them said. "You don't fuck with Army intel and get away with it."

"What the hell are you talking about?" I said.

"Hitting the Captain with a shotgun. Then blowing up his boat. With him in it. That's what I'm talking about."

I needed to stall for time so Rodney could get there.

"I didn't have anything to do with that," I said as I struggled. "I don't know shit about explosives."

"Just like you didn't have anything to do with those cops rousting us," said the guy who was holding me. "Come on, let's finish this and go home," he said to his partner.

I braced myself for the first blow, tightening my stomach muscles, an effort that hurt like hell from the previous beat-down. Come on, Rodney.

The glare of headlights turned into the alley from the end I was facing. My assailants turned their attention away from me towards the oncoming vehicle. But the one guy held on tightly, so I couldn't break free.

The vehicle moved slowly in our direction, its tires crunching on the alleyway's cinder paving. It wasn't Rodney. My car didn't have halogen headlights. It stopped moving towards us. All we could see were those headlights on full bright.

The vehicle door opened. In the glow of the dome light a shadowy figure exited the vehicle. The door closed, and the light went out. Nothing but headlights again. The Army guys froze. I stared at the guy who had been positioned to hit me. He was looking over his shoulder at the headlights. A quiet "phoot!" sounded accompanied by a flash of light from alongside the vehicle. I recognized the sound of a weapon with a silencer. The guy in front of me got a surprised look, eyes and mouth wide open. He fell to the pavement, his eyes staring into nothing, and he was motionless.

The other guy released me and started to run away towards the other end of the alley. "Phoot!" He went down with a small, blood-stained hole in the back of his uniform jacket.

I fumbled with my crutches to try to shield myself in the doorway in case I was to be next. But the vehicle door opened and closed, and the vehicle peeled rubber. Its engine roared as it backed rapidly out of the alley, the car and its occupant obscured by the bright headlights.

I leaned against the wall to wait for Rodney and looked at the two dead Army guys. This was going to be a lot of paperwork.

Rodney drove up soon and stopped short of the scene. He got out of the car and stared at the corpses.

"Uncle Stanley! You okay? What the hell happened here?"

"I'm okay," I said. I punched the direct phone number for the homicide unit into my cell phone. "Pick up my gun for me. It's over there."

"Did you shoot those two guys?" he asked.

"No. I had a guardian angel."

"That might explain what I saw."

"What?"

"As I turned onto the side street a black SUV went screaming past behind me."

"Did you get a license number?"

"No."

"Good."

Chapter 19

We stayed with the bodies until the cops came. Then Rodney helped me up the stairs. I went into my office and put my gun in the safe. I got the bottle out of the desk drawer and was on my second drink when Bill Penrod walked into the office. He sat across from me and looked at me for a while, shaking his head. I poured him a drink. He took out his notepad and a pencil that was only about three inches long.

"USACIDC is on the way," he said.

"What's that mean?" Rodney asked.

"US Army Criminal Investigation Command," I said.

"What's the 'D' for?" Rodney said.

"Nobody knows," Bill said with a smile. "They call themselves CID. Go figure. They'll want jurisdiction, it being their guys that got shot."

"Are they investigating the boat explosion too?" I asked.

"No. It was a civilian boat, and no body parts were found. They don't get interested until there's some evidence."

He took a drink and said, "So, Stan, what happened here?"

I told him what little I could. Rodney sat at his own desk and, for the first time in his life, kept his mouth shut until spoken to.

Bill asked him, "Can you tell me what kind of SUV it was?"

"One of the bigger ones," Rodney said. "It was dark and I couldn't see the emblems. They all look alike anyway."

His mail-order badge had arrived that morning, and he wore it on his belt. He sat such that everyone could see it.

"How about a license number?" Bill asked.

"No, sir. Too dark and it sped by too fast."

"How many occupants?"

"I couldn't tell."

"And I guess you didn't get a look at the driver?"

"No, sir."

Bill put his notepad away and took the final swig of his drink. I poured him another.

"Where's that CID guy?" he said. "I want to go home. You know, the unit called me because you and I have history. I was almost home. Had to turn around and come back." He looked behind him at the door. "Where the fuck is CID?"

"I was hoping you'd stay a while, Bill," I said. "Help me from having to go on base for an interrogation."

"Who do you think did it, Stan?"

"I don't have a clue."

But I had a hunch. Buford had said he'd get Sanford to deal with the Army guys. My guess was that either Sanford himself or one of his Men in Black had saved me. The black SUV fit my scenario.

As we talked, the outer door opened and three men in civilian clothes walked in. Rodney shifted in his chair so they could see his badge.

"Sergeant Penrod?" one of them asked.

"That's me," Bill said. "You guys USACIDC?"

"We are, sir," he said. "I'm special agent Stewart."

"You guys want a drink," I asked.

"No, sir," Stewart said. "We're on duty."

"How come you guys don't have a TV show like NCIS?" Rodney asked.

"Too many letters," Stewart said.

Penrod said, "This is Stanley Bentworth and his nephew Rodney. They witnessed the shooting. You guys take over, and I can go home now."

"Not quite," Stewart said. "We're not taking jurisdiction."

"Why not?" Penrod asked.

"Your two stiffs aren't ours."

"What do you mean not yours?"

"They aren't Army personnel. No dog tags, no ID, no insignia, bad haircuts, and the wrong kind of shoes. Those guys were pretending to be Army. Even the uniforms aren't standard issue. Probably from a costume store."

Bill said, "Stan, how come you didn't notice all that?"

"I was too busy getting the shit beat out of me to notice details," I said. "What about the car? It looks real."

"That is ours," he said. "Signed out to Captain Pugh. If you don't mind, Sergeant Penrod, we'll take the car now. The keys are in it."

"Damn!" Penrod said. "I was hoping to go home sometime tonight. No, I don't mind. You can take it."

"Wait," I said. "Couldn't those guys be Army Intelligence? Under cover? They were working for Captain Pugh, who is, I believe, Army Intelligence."

"Was," Stewart said. "He was Army Intelligence. Nobody's seen Jeremy since his boat blew up. So, as far as we're concerned, if he isn't dead, he's AWOL. And if those two guys lying in the street out there were ours, we'd know them. Nope. Not our jurisdiction. We're out of here. It's all yours. Here's our card. Call if anything changes."

He passed out cards to Bill, Rodney, and me. With that, the three agents turned and left.

"Shit," Penrod said. "So much for getting home on time. Stan, I'll need your piece for a ballistics match. I'll get it back to you after the lab eliminates it as the murder weapon."

I went to the safe to get Roscoe. Now Rodney knew where I kept it. I took the pistol out of the holster, gave it to Bill, and sat down.

Everyone left and we closed shop. This time, I had Rodney walk in front of me while I groped my way down the stairs without help. One more hurdle cleared. We went out the front door to avoid the crime scene. I walked with him to the car. He started to get in the driver's side, but I said, "I'll drive."

The drive back to Amanda's house was okay. I managed to work the shifter and pedals even though I still had casts on.

When we got to Amanda's house, I told Rodney, "I'm going home. You get your room back. Thanks for all your help."

"No problem."

Why do people always say that? Whatever happened to "you're welcome?" If there had been a problem, does it mean they wouldn't have done it? I wonder about shit like that.

"Tell your mom thanks too. I'll see you at work tomorrow. Bring my clothes and shaving kit."

I drove home and managed my way from the parking lot into my apartment. I called Bunny at the diner and invited her over.

"Bring supper," I said.

Things were looking up.

Chapter 20

I started my investigation into Vitole's murder at his house the next morning. His widow answered the door. She was startled by my appearance. All the bandages and bruises. Nothing like having a mummy on a crutch show up at your front door. That's right, I was down to one crutch. It was like being released from bonds. I had my good hand free.

Stella Vitole was as I remembered her. Plump and unattractive. Like many such ladies, she overdid it with makeup, hairdo, and perfume trying to compensate, trying to be young again. Some people refuse to age gracefully. Others have no graceful beginnings from which to age. I should talk.

I introduced myself. "Mrs. Vitole, I am detective Bentworth. I am investigating your husband's murder."

I flashed my P.I. badge. She barely glanced at it. The shiny gold shield had done its job. She thought I was a cop on the job, and I let her think it.

She said, "A Sergeant Penrod already took my statement."

"I know. This is just some follow-up."

"Do you work with Sergeant Penrod?" she asked.

"I did before he made Sergeant." Not a lie, but not exactly truthful either.

"Please come in."

She led me to the living room, the same room where I had delivered a veiled threat to her husband.

"Please sit down," she said. "How did you injure yourself?"

"In the line of duty. A different case."

I sat on the sofa, careful not to bump my casts on anything.

"Can I get you something?"

"No, ma'am, I'm fine." I took out my notepad and pencil. "You told Sergeant Penrod that your husband said you and he would be coming into some money related to Buford Overbee?"

She sat in the chair and looked at me.

"Yes, I did. And now you people have him charged with my husband's murder. That was really fast. My congratulations and appreciation."

"I'll pass your comments on to the sergeant. Do you know your neighbors, the Sproleses? Your husband's murder happened in front of their house, I believe."

She got quiet and looked out the plate glass window into her back yard. Then she said, "Yes. We used to be friends."

"Used to be? Aren't you still friends?"

"No. Marsha and I had a falling out."

"What was the nature of that falling out."

"I'd rather not discuss it," she said.

"Well, this is a murder investigation. If there's something I should know..."

"Perhaps you should ask her, detective."

"I will. Have you returned to work yet?"

"No. I will soon. My employer has been understanding throughout all this."

"Where do you work in case I need to contact you during the day?"

"The Arnold Locksmith and Security Company in town. Here's a card with the phone number."

"The falling out you had with Mrs. Sproles. It wasn't about her and your husband's affair, was it?"

That took her by surprise. She took a while to answer.

"I don't know what you are talking about, detective. I just buried my husband. What kind of question is that?"

"Just trying to get all our ducks lined up, ma'am."

"Well, line them up somewhere else. I want you to leave now."

I thanked her, got no "you're welcome" in return, not even a "no problem," and went out to my car.

The Sproles house, two doors up, was almost the identical model as the Vitole house. I rang the doorbell and waited. A woman answered the door.

"Yes?"

Marsha Sproles was a pretty woman in her mid-thirties. The pictures I had of her didn't do her justice. She was standing in a darkened doorway when I took them, and she had just come from a roll in the hay.

Today she wore a house dress that neither flaunted nor hid her trim figure. Her brunette hair was pinned up, and she wore just a hint of blush and lipstick. The all-American girl next door. I couldn't blame Vitole for going for her.

She too reacted to my appearance. What was this battle-worn, beat-up, and bandaged guy doing on her doorstep? Certainly not selling Girl Scout cookies.

"Mrs. Sproles. I'm detective Bentworth." I flashed the badge. It worked again.

"How can I help you?" she asked.

"This is about the murder of your neighbor, Mario Vitole."

She got a pained look on her face. I couldn't interpret its meaning.

"Yes. Terrible, wasn't it?"

"I need to talk to you about the murder taking place in front of your house. Do you know why he was there?"

"No."

A lie. We both knew why he was there. Except she didn't know I knew.

"I was in the house and heard the shot," she said. "I ran and looked out the door. He was lying in the street."

"How long from when you heard the shot until you saw the body?"

"Less than a minute. I had something on the stove and had to turn it down."

What presence of mind. Tend to the soup, and then go see why there's a corpse in the street in front of your house. I didn't pursue the illogic of that.

"Did you see anyone else out there?" I asked.

"No. The other policeman already asked all these questions."

"Yes, ma'am. Sometimes a witness recalls details they had overlooked before. It's routine to do a follow-up interview."

"That makes sense," she said. "Would you like some coffee? Or tea?"

"No thank you," I said.

She got up to pour herself a cup of coffee. I wished she'd have offered a drink. But then I'd have had to do the I'm-on-duty routine, so what would be the point?

"Mrs. Vitole said that you and she have had a recent falling out. Is that true?"

She let go of a big sigh as if I had just opened a door that ought to be left closed. "I suppose you could call it that," she said. "Stella's a jealous woman. She thought Mario and I were having an affair."

Bingo. The affair is in the air.

"Were you?"

"Of course not."

"Did your husband share her suspicions?"

"I don't think so." Now her voice was worried. "I think he would have said something."

"Where was he when the shooting took place?"

"At work."

"Where does he work?"

"Arnold Locksmith and Security."

Things were starting to fall into place. That was interesting. And maybe relevant. The husband of the adulteress and the wife of the cheating husband and victim worked together.

"With Mrs. Vitole," I said.

"Yes. He hired Stella last year as dispatcher. To dispatch the service trucks."

"Is Mr. Sproles a locksmith?"

I needed a suspect who could open the trunk of a Rolls Royce.

"No. He's general manager."

"Does he have other duties besides management?"

"Sometimes when they're shorthanded, William goes on service calls."

"So he does have locksmith skills."

"Not at a very technical level. He can install locks and fix alarm systems and like that."

"Can he pick a lock?" The sixty-four dollar question.

"I don't think so. Why do you ask?"

"Just gathering information. Now, did you say that you saw a Rolls Royce parked at Mr. Vitole's house earlier that same day?"

"Yes, I did."

"Why did you think that was significant?"

"The other detective asked me if I'd seen anything unusual. A Rolls Royce parked in this neighborhood is unusual. That's all."

It was time to spring it on her.

"Ma'am, are you aware that Mr. Vitole had a snapshot of the two of you embracing in your doorway?"

"What? What snapshot? What do you mean? Have you seen such a snapshot?"

"Do you think Mrs. Vitole might have found it and shared it with your husband?"

"What are you suggesting? You people caught the man who killed Mario. That big shot financier. It was on the news. Why are you out here—"

"Just some routine follow-up, Mrs. Sproles. I'll be in touch if anything comes up."

Chapter 21

Investigating a murder means pissing people off. Maybe you get to apologize later, but for the most part you interrogate people, suggest one form of involvement or another, and watch for their reactions to form instincts about who the bad guys are. If it works right, the practice points you in a direction that helps you close the case. Which makes pissing people off worth it.

I had just pissed off two ladies in a nice neighborhood, one who had recently become a widow and the other who had been cheating on her husband. Now I was about to piss off the husband.

Arnold Locksmith and Security was on the edge of the wrong side of town. Not a place you'd want to leave your expensive car parked. It didn't worry me. Nobody would steal my car. If anything, they'd leave me another one just like it.

The one-story building was a half block long and wide. Behind it a parking lot held about five vans with the company's logo on the side, the same logo that decorated the front of the building over the main entrance. The logo was the only part of the business that looked elegant.

The receptionist greeted me with a nice smile. She was a teenager, maybe just out of school. Or a dropout. I showed her my badge.

"Whoa!" she said, even though I wasn't moving. Except to put the badge away before somebody saw what it was.

"Can I help you?" Her name tag said Pamela.

"I need to see your duty roster, Pamela," I said.

"My what?" You'd think I'd asked to see her underwear.

"Your log of when employees work and where they're assigned. I'm investigating a murder."

"Oh, you mean Mrs. Vitole's husband?"

"That's the one. Can I see the roster?"

"We don't have one. Do you want to talk to the general manager?"

"Not yet. You seem like a bright girl. Maybe you can tell me. Was anyone in your company absent from work the day Mr. Vitole got shot?"

She typed on her computer and said, "Everybody was here that day."

"Mrs. Vitole too?"

"Yes. Until the policeman came to tell her."

That gave Stella an alibi. One less suspect.

"How about when somebody goes out. Without a duty roster how do you keep track of where everybody is?"

"We keep a record of the service orders."

"Was Mr. Sproles in the office that day?"

She referred to the monitor. "No. He took one of the trucks out for a service call."

"Can you make me a copy of the service order?"

"Sure." She printed the document and gave it to me. I folded it and put it in my pocket.

"Is Mr. Sproles here now?"

"That's the door to his office."

"Thank you, Pamela," I said.

I knocked.

"Come in," a man's voice said.

I opened the door and went into William Sproles's office.

Sproles was middle aged, balding, and every bit the couch potato I saw from across the street the other day.

"You'd be detective Bentworth," Sproles said. "My wife called and said you were at our house. Please sit. I wouldn't want you to fall down in my office."

He seemed pissed. She must have told him what I'd asked her.

He didn't ask to see my badge, and I didn't offer it.

I sat in an uncomfortable folding chair, the best his office had to offer for guests. I guessed that he didn't close many sales here.

"Mr. Sproles, where were you the morning Mario Vitole was killed?"

"I was here. Working."

"Think back carefully, sir. That's not what your girl Pamela said."

"What Pamela said? How would she know where I was that many days ago? She can't even remember where the coffee room is."

"She looked up your work orders. You were out on a service call."

"Well, if you already know that, why ask me? I probably just mixed up my days."

"Not many people would forget where they were when their neighbor was gunned down in front of their own house."

He glared at me for a moment. "If you don't have any more questions, detective, I have work to do."

"One more. Did you see the picture that Vitole had of him kissing your wife in your doorway one day while you were at work?"

"Whatever are you talking about?"

"I'm talking about the affair that your wife was having with the dead man. I'm talking about the proof of that affair that Mrs. Vitole had and probably showed you. I'm talking about you not having an alibi for the time of the murder. Do you want me to keep talking?"

I really wished Bill Penrod was here. He'd have had this guy pissing himself to confess long before now. All I was doing was pissing him off.

"No, I don't think you should keep talking," Sproles said. "I think you should leave now. I know my rights. I don't have to talk to you."

He was right. Even if I was a cop, he didn't have to talk to me. I wasn't getting anywhere. But his reaction to the story about the affair was telling. He wasn't shocked, surprised or outraged. The affair wasn't news to him.

"Thank you for your time, Mr. Sproles," I said. I pulled myself out of the metal chair and went out and towards the main door. Sproles came out of his office and spoke to Pamela. He was probably chewing her ass about the service orders.

The next stop was the home of the customer on Sproles's service order for the day of the murder. A lady came to the door.

"Good afternoon ma'am. I represent the Arnold Security company. This is just a follow-up courtesy call to make sure you were happy with our recent service call."

"Service call? I don't recall any service call."

I showed her the service order. "Didn't you have one of our technicians here to repair your alarm system?"

"No. I'm sorry, there must be some mistake."

"Probably a clerical error," I said. "I'm sorry to have troubled you."

I returned to my car and left.

Sproles was caught in a lie. He wasn't where he said he'd been that day. He'd probably fabricated the service order to account for his absence. Its relevance to the murder of his neighbor wasn't clear, however. Many valid reasons could have a fellow taking time off work under false pretenses. Maybe he was interviewing for another job. Maybe he snuck away to go to a ball game. Or maybe he too had a lady friend on the side.

It's a complicated world. Nothing is ever cut and dried.

Chapter 22

I stopped at Ray's for lunch, took my usual seat in a booth, and waited. After a while, the cook, who was Ray the owner, stuck his head out of the kitchen and said, "In the ladies room. She'll be out soon."

I waited for several minutes more. A couple came in and took a seat. They had to wait too. After five more minutes, the fellow called out, "Is this place open for business?"

Ray came out and took their order. He looked at me and shrugged. Then he came over to my table.

"You know what you want?" he asked.

"A burger and some fries, Ray. And coffee."

On his way back to the kitchen, Ray stopped at the ladies room door and pounded. "Come on out, Bunny. You have customers."

The bathroom door opened, and Bunny came out. She looked at me, and then away. She took water and tableware to the other party.

Ray called out, "Order up," and Bunny went to get my burger. She brought it over and put it in front of me. Then she turned to walk away without saying anything.

This was the lady I slept with last night and intended to sleep with tonight. And she acted like I was wearing an AIDS medical alert bracelet.

"Hey!" I said. "What's the idea."

"Order up!" Ray called.

"I have to get this order," she said and hurried away.

When I finished my burger, I waited again. I could have tossed the money on the table and left. I could have walked out on the check. But I waited. After about a half hour, she came over and took my money.

"You want to tell me what's going on?" I said when she brought the change. "As if I didn't know."

"What do you mean?" she said, still not looking me in the face.

"Come on, Bunny. I know the heave-ho when I see it. We've done it enough times already. Who is it this time?"

She sat down across from me.

"I don't want to hurt you," she said.

"Since when?"

"I don't. But here it is." She paused and looked out the window. "Barry is back. He wants to go out with me again."

"Then do it," I said. "Just do it. But this is it."

"It? You mean I'll never see you again? We can't stay friends like before?"

"Oh, you'll see me. Ray makes too good a burger. I'm cutting you out, not Ray. From now on, Bunny, you're just the waitress. Bring my food, take my money, and just don't talk to me. I can't do this anymore."

I left her crying, went back to the office, and gave my notebook to Rodney.

"Copy these notes to the whiteboard," I said. "I take good notes, so you shouldn't need much translation. If you don't understand something, mark it and ask me about it tomorrow."

I got the bottle from the desk drawer and left without saying anything more to Willa or Rodney. She knew better than to ask what was wrong. She'd seen me through the same thing enough times before.

I threw the bottle in my car for later and went to Oliver's for now. Sammy was on duty, my friend, my shoulder to cry on, my ear to bend. There were a few customers there. I limped up to the bar and hoisted my broken body onto a barstool.

"What the hell happened to you?" Sammy asked. He pushed a tumbler of a double Jack neat in front of me.

"Got beat up by two guys."

"On a case?" he asked. He was drying glasses from the washer and putting them on a glass shelf behind the bar.

"Yeah. A couple mokes playing soldier."

"You sure do look like shit."

"I get that all the time."

"You charge extra for getting beat up?"

"Pro bono. Helping my sister."

"Ain't that always the way?"

I knocked back the double and pushed the glass across to him.

"You need some pain killers, Stan? I got some good stuff. Muscle relaxers."

"Pour."

He filled the glass. Sammy's doubles were more like triples, and it didn't take long for them to take a guy down.

"Drinking heavy tonight?"

"Yeah. Got problems."

"With the beat-down?"

"No."

"The problem named Bunny?" Sammy had helped me through this mess a couple times before. He knew the signs.

"It is. Just when you think everything's kosher, she yanks the rug."

"Why do you put up with it, Stan?"

"I don't know. Best blow job in town might be a good reason."

He finished drying his last tumbler and went down the bar to refill a draft beer for another customer. Then he came back.

"How do you know she's the best blow job in town? Have you had all the blow jobs in town?"

"Had my share," I said. "Bunny's the best. Of course, the worst one I ever had was wonderful."

I pushed the tumbler across again, he poured.

"So what are you telling me?" Sammy asked. "You fell in love with a blow job?"

"You would too. Bunny's nickname is 'the Spoiler.'"

"How's that?"

"Once she's waxed your carrot, you're spoiled for anyone else."

"The Spoiler. That's pretty good. But you've had some nice ladies. What happened to that wife you had? She wasn't around very long either."

"That was Brenda. Divorce. I met her when we were both on the rebound. We only knew each other about two months."

"She sure was easy on the eyes."

"She was. I couldn't believe such a lovely peach would have me."

"You're always hard on yourself," Sammy said.

"She didn't stay lovely for long. Turns out she had a split personality, and both of them gave me shit every day of the week."

He laughed. "That's a joke, right?"

"Nothing funny about it. One night she broke a whiskey bottle on the sink and threw it at me. Twenty stitches in my arm. The scar's under this cast or I'd show it to you. Anyway, that did it. Some things cannot be forgiven. That was expensive whiskey."

Sammy laughed at my portrayal of love gone awry.

"She took everything we had," I said, "which wasn't much, leaving me only this watch."

"Quite the heirloom."

"Yeah, a real collector's item. She told the judge I should have done better by her, should've made sure we'd have more assets that she could take."

"Didn't you have any defense at all?"

"I used my P.I. skills and made candid videos of her *in flagrante delicto*."

"What's that?"

"Fucking another guy. I tell you, Sammy, she had talent between the sheets. Those videos would have been too hardcore for the Internet. The judge gave her everything she wanted."

"What happened to the videos?"

"The judge kept them."

Sammy laughed so hard he started coughing.

"Don't get married, Sammy," I said when he quieted down. "Don't set yourself up for that divorce shit. Just find a woman who hates you and buy her a house."

"I've heard that one."

"I've lived it." I emptied the glass and pushed it over.

"You driving?" Sammy asked.

"I am."

"This is the last one, then," he said. "Unless you want me to call you a cab."

"I've been called worse."

Sammy leaned on the bar. "You don't want to get pulled over."

"That's okay. With these crutches I couldn't walk a straight line anyway. Put this on the tab. How much is it?"

"National debt," he said.

"Okay. I'll have Willa get square with you. We got a windfall."

"Some advice, Stan. Don't be so quick to take the Spoiler back. She knows you're always there for her. Let her find out what it's like to not have you in reserve."

"Easier said than done." I leaned back and sighed. "The Spoiler."

"Well then, pal, ignore my advice. It's better for my business. You quit drowning your sorrows, and I go on Food Stamps."

He moved to another part of the bar to talk to a couple of customers. I took my time drinking the last drink.

A fellow I didn't know came in and sat next to me at the bar. I hoped he wasn't looking to pick me up. I wasn't that desperate.

"Mr. Bentworth?" he said.

I turned and looked at him. He was bigger than me—who wasn't—and well-dressed. His nose was bent. Uh-oh.

"Who wants to know?" I said. That's what they always say in cowboy movies.

"My name is not important."

Nobody wants to tell me their name.

"Maybe you should get an important name. Might help with your self-esteem issues."

He was not moved by my humor. He continued. "My sources tell me you might know the whereabouts of an old friend."

"I don't have any old friends. Or any young ones."

"My old friend," he said. "I'm looking for him, and I have reason to believe he might be living around here under an assumed name."

"Is that better than an unimportant name?"

No matter how I tried, I couldn't get a laugh out of this guy.

"His name used to be Tony Curro. You know him?"

"Nope. Never heard of him."

"I figured that's what you'd say. How did you hurt yourself?"

"Discount bungee jumping."

He lowered his voice. "Well, you understand, if you know my friend and don't tell me, your next jump will be without the bungee."

"Why do you think I know him?"

"No reason I shouldn't tell you. We got an anonymous tip saying I should look you up. That's all he'd tell me."

That could only have been Vitole after I visited him. I hadn't given him my name. He must've gotten my license number and had it traced.

Now I understood why Vitole had ignored my warning and demanded that Buford put the twenty grand back. If he got rid of me without outing Buford, his money train would keep rolling. Assuming I didn't cave in and give Buford up.

All I could do for this fellow was lie. "I can't help you. I really don't know the guy you're looking for."

"Well, my family gave me the job of finding Curro. This is as far as I've gotten, and all I found is you. Here's a card with my cell phone. If you think of anything, call. If I don't hear from you soon, I might have to come calling again."

He got up and went out the front door.

Buford got it right when he said my ass would be in the cross-hairs if the mob found out we were connected. I wondered how many of his relatives this guy had told about me.

I called Rodney.

"Get your laptop going and find the GPS for this number," I said. I read the number to him and then said, "When you find where it is, call Overbee. I'll let him know to expect your call."

"You got it, Uncle Stanley."

"No, I don't yet, but I expect to."

I called Buford.

"Remember when you told me the mob would be on me?"

"Yes. What happened?"

"I just had a visit. I got his cell phone number. Rodney will be calling you with his location."

"Not to worry, Stan. We'll take care of it."

My crutches and I limped out to the car. It was almost sup-pertime, but I wasn't hungry, I wasn't up for seeing Bunny, and I sure wasn't going to eat anything I cooked myself. Not in this shape.

I drove home, took the bottle into the apartment, and drank myself to sleep.

Chapter 23

The next morning I was in the office, back to normal, which was needing a shave, bleary-eyed, with a star-spangled hangover and yet another resolve to quit drinking. I sent Willa out for some V8 and vodka, Buford's hangover cure. I sat staring at the wall until she came back, whereupon I drank two coffee cups full of the potion. Drinking a hangover cure isn't the same as drinking, I told myself.

I told Willa to call Oliver's for a total on my tab and to send them a check.

"And no lectures on what I'm spending, either," I told her. "Some guys collect cars, others play golf. I count cigarette burns on the bar at Oliver's."

"How many are there?" she asked.

"Several more as of last night."

"Get to work," she said. "Earn your keep."

I went into my office. Rodney was already there.

"I located that cell phone at an Italian restaurant in town, Uncle Stanley."

"Did you call Overbee?"

"Yep. He called this morning and said to tell you the problem has been taken care of. Who's Sanford?"

"The guy who takes care of problems. Let's get to work."

Rodney's transcriptions of my notes onto the whiteboard were good. I had to make a couple of corrections, and they were due to my crappy handwriting.

"Here's things to add," I said to Rodney when he came in. "From memory. Put all this wherever it fits on the board."

Rodney listened and transcribed my summary with dates and events posted on the timeline.

"Willa," I called out to the outer office. "Would you go across the street and get me some breakfast? The V8 is starting to work."

"Sure," she called back.

Willa left, and I continued to recite things for Rodney to post on the whiteboard.

My cell phone rang. It was the pay phone at Ray's Diner on the caller ID. Had to be Bunny.

"What?" I said.

"Stan, I'm sorry." She was still kind of weepy.

"Apology noted. Have a good time on your date."

I hung up the cell phone.

Willa came in with breakfast. "Was that what I thought it was?" she asked.

"Depends on what you thought it was," I said.

"Sounded like you blowing off Bunny. That's long overdue."

"Willa, I don't need Dear Abby just now."

"Yes, you do," she said with a firm tone. "You don't want my advice, but here it is for what it's worth."

I started to interrupt, but she said, "Shut up and listen. She'll beg you to take her back but don't do it. Not right away. That's what she's counting on. Good old Stan, always there when she needs him, always in reserve. She's keeping you in the bank for when times are slow."

That was what Sammy had said.

"Willa—"

"She needs to learn that you never know what you have until you've lost it. I never appreciated my husband while he was here."

Willa's husband had died a while back.

"And quit getting drunk over it. That doesn't get a woman back. It sure doesn't keep her. As you should know by now."

"End of lecture?" I asked.

"For now," she said.

I shook my head and turned back to the whiteboard.

"What's left?" I asked Rodney.

"I think that covers it, Uncle Stanley. What are you going to do next?"

"I'm going to see if I can question the four suspects that live with Buford."

"Can I go along and observe?"

"No. That doesn't work. An interrogation team works in sync. We know by instinct from working together what questions each other will ask and when. We know when one should step down and the other take over. We complement each other."

"Sure. Good cop, bad cop. I know how that works. I watch TV."

"You aren't ready for that, and private investigation rarely uses those techniques anyway. We don't work murder cases. The only reason we have this one is the cops think they got it closed, and we think they got it wrong."

"What can I do?"

"Stay here at your computer and collect everything you can find on Sanford, Ramon, Missy, and Serena. I got no background on any of them except that Sanford used to be a lawyer with the mob, and Ramon is an illegal alien."

Rodney was typing on his laptop, making notes.

"One more thing. Vitole was shaking down other guys in witness protection. Maybe one of them bumped him off. Get into the Marshals site, and do a search. Pull the names of witness protection clients who have relocated somewhere around here and are still alive. If we can point suspicion at any upstanding citizens like that, maybe we can create reasonable doubt for Buford."

Chapter 24

I went again to Buford's residence for the hard part, interrogating the client's friends and family. Buford was on the patio in his bathing trunks. The ankle bracelet had chafed the skin on his shin just above his foot as he'd said. His ankle was big like the rest of him. The bracelet was in its largest buckle setting and, even so, pinched his skin.

"Your nephew seems to be good at hacking into shit," he said. "You think he can get this thing off me?"

"Maybe. One time he took the boot off his car's wheel that the cops had put on."

"That's good. What did he do with it?"

"He changed the pins in the tumbler lock so they couldn't open it. Then he put the boot on a police cruiser parked in front of a doughnut shop."

"Man, that kid has balls. What kind of trouble did that get him in?"

"I intervened. He got community service and no record."

"You're a good uncle."

"I am."

"So, what about this bracelet?"

"I'll ask him."

I doubted that Rodney could do much about the bracelet. They go out of their way to make them tamper-proof.

"Thanks for taking care of that wise guy," I said.

"Thank Sanford."

"You think I'll get more visits?"

"Not likely. He probably didn't tell anyone about you. They usually wait until the job is done. Don't bother the bosses with details. Just results."

That was a huge relief. It wasn't a guarantee, but if anyone knew how the mob operated, Buford did.

"I need a private place to talk to your people," I said.

"How about my study? If they don't cooperate, you can take a gun off the wall and shoot them."

I went into the study and sat at the giant desk. While I waited for my first interrogation subject, I called Rodney.

"You think you can remove a house arrest ankle bracelet without triggering its alarm?"

"I don't know, Uncle Stanley. I'd have to look at it."

"Next chance you get, make an appointment to come see Mr. Overbee. If you can do it, there'll be a bonus."

Buford sent Ramon in first.

"Ramon," I said. "Sit down." He did. "I am collecting information related to where everyone was when Mr. Vitole got shot. Where were you that morning?"

"I was here all day, Señor. Sanford and I were playing pool."

"Who won?"

"Sanford did. It is advisable to let Sanford win."

"Mr. Overbee says you play chess. Can you beat Sanford at that?"

"He will not play me."

"You're very loyal to Mr. Overbee."

"Si, Señor. He is my benefactor. He is trying to get me a green card and eventually citizenship."

"So you'd do anything to protect him."

"Anything."

"Did you know he was having problems with Mr. Vitole?"

"No, I did not. I knew he was having problems with someone."

"Weren't you here the day I told him about Mr. Vitole?"

"Si, Señor, I was here, but I do not listen when Señor Overbee discusses business."

"Thank you, Ramon. That's all I have for now. Bring me black coffee, please."

Ramon left and Missy came in.

"Dad's got us lined up out there like in a doctor's waiting room."

"Miss Curro, where were you the morning Mr. Vitole was shot?"

"Serena and I were shopping."

"Okay. I don't need you to prove it to me, but if the cops ask, is there anyway you can substantiate where you were?"

"They can ask Serena."

"Yeah, but you are each other's alibi. They'd want corroborating evidence."

"Easy. Look at my Dad's credit card account. Serena practically bought out Belksdales."

"And you?"

"I didn't even buy lunch. But Serena will tell you I was with her."

Missy left, and Ramon came in and put a pot of coffee and a cup on the table. He poured me a cup and left.

Usually in a situation like this, the tendency is to cut corners, save time, and not interview a corroborating witness. I would expect Serena to say what Missy said she would say. But experience had taught me to expect the unexpected. And, besides, it was Serena. I wasn't going to miss an opportunity to look at her again. I asked her to come in.

The young woman was so beautiful that I found it difficult to concentrate. She was wearing that same bikini with the white terrycloth robe hanging off her shoulders. When she sat, she crossed her legs so that the robe fell off them such that they were on full display to her best advantage. I am a weak man. I was ready to believe anything she said. I have to work on that.

"So you're a detective," she said. "That must be like exciting."

She uncrossed her legs and re-crossed them the other way. Be still my heart.

"No, it's mostly boring routine work."

"Well, I'm impressed. Some day you'll have to tell me some of your stories."

Take a deep breath. Relax. Down to business.

"Serena, I understand that you went shopping the day of the murder."

"What day was that?" she asked.

What woman could forget the day a murder happened of which her husband had been accused? I told her the date.

"That's too long ago. I don't know where I was." She flicked a bit of lint off her shoulder and looked into my eyes. Fortunately I was looking at her face at the time and not other places that were demanding my attention. She smiled. I smiled back. The gaze took longer than it should have. Then I snapped out of it and continued.

"It would be the day you went to Belksdales with Missy."

"Oh, that day. I decided at the last minute to like go out. I was in town the whole day from when Buford got home."

"And Missy was with you?"

"Not the whole day. She like doesn't get up that early."

"When did she join you?"

"For lunch. There's this really chic little vegetarian restaurant in the town square. All kinds of, y'know, mushroom dishes and cheese soups. We ate there."

"And you didn't see her before that?"

"No."

"Did you drive yourself into town?"

"No. Ramon drove me. I don't like to drive in traffic."

"Did he stay with you all day?"

"No, he waits in the car. And he returned here just before lunch to get Missy. After he dropped her off, I guess he was, y'know, in the car. He like picked us up later to bring us home."

I wrote what she said in my notebook.

"Mr. Bentworth, you are going to like find out who killed that man, aren't you?"

"I'm going to try."

"And Buford will be y'know cleared?"

"I hope so."

"So do I. Buford and I are true soul mates like ever since we met."

"Where did you meet?"

"I was a dancer at a club in Philadelphia. He knew the owner who introduced us. We both knew immediately that we were y'know meant for each other. Ever since then we've been like two stones that pass in the night."

She said that just as I was taking a swallow of coffee. The coffee shot out of my nose and went down my shirtfront. I grabbed a napkin and sopped it up. I suppressed my laughter and asked her to send Sanford in.

Serena's story had sent three alibis out the window. Ramon wasn't where he said he was. Neither was Missy. Sanford's alibi depended on Ramon's. And if the store receipts didn't bear her out, Serena had nothing to back up her story either. My gut instinct was right. Always get statements from everybody even when you think you know what they'll say. They can surprise you.

One more to go. Sanford came in. I had saved him for last. He'd be the toughest one to read.

"Sanford, where were you when the murder went down?"

"Here."

"All day?"

"Yes."

"Can anybody vouch for that?"

"Ramon can."

Always let the subject know he's been caught in a lie. His reaction to that can tell you a lot.

"That's what he said too," I said, watching Sanford closely. "But I've also been told that he drove the ladies into town that morning and was away from here until the afternoon."

Sanford did not answer. He just sat and looked at me.

"Can you explain why he'd say that?" I asked after waiting for the response that didn't come.

"Yes."

"What's the explanation?"

"The four of us need to get our stories straight."

Another surprise. He had just admitted that their alibis were contrived to account for a period of time that none of them could account for.

His answer also revealed that he didn't give a shit what they told me. I'm not the cops.

"By the way," I said. "Thanks for fixing that wise guy problem I had. I owe you."

"Don't know what you're talking about."

"Understood. That's about it. Could you find Mr. Overbee and ask him to come in?"

Sanford left and Buford came in, settled in a chair, and got a drink from Ramon.

"Buford," I said, "everybody tells a different story. As near as I can tell, the only one who isn't lying is Serena."

"She's too dumb to lie," he said. "That's what I love about her. Among other things."

"Well, the result is that I got nothing to eliminate any of them except maybe Serena from the likely suspect list."

"You got to crawl before you can walk," he said. "One step at a time." His mixed metaphors told me that my lack of success with the interrogations didn't bother him.

"Do you have all the credit card receipts for that day? It'll tell us whether Serena was shopping in the morning."

"Yeah, she keeps everything."

He got up and went out of the office. After a few minutes he came back in leafing through a handful of cash register receipts.

"Jesus Christ," he said. "Not only do I have the mob and the cops on me, but Citibank is going to be coming after me too."

I took the receipts from him and checked the time stamps. Serena was exonerated.

On the drive back to the office I went over the four interrogations in my head. What would Bill Penrod have done that I didn't do? I tried to recall how we bounced off one another during an interrogation. I'd proceed as I had today, and then, at every inconsistency in a suspect's story, Bill would jump in, yell at them, accuse them of the crime, and demand that they change their story and come clean or face arrest for obstruction, lying to a cop, impeding an investigation, or any one of a number of charges that he could cite or make up. He'd intimidate witnesses until they either broke down or convinced him that they didn't do it. If they did neither, he'd fall back and let me take over again.

That's what Bill would have done. I'm not like that. I was always the good cop. Besides, this time I was questioning the people on our side. It was a confusing dichotomy.

Chapter 25

Ray's Diner wouldn't be crowded this time of day. The lunch rush was over, and dinner wasn't for a few more hours. I stopped to get a quick burger on my way back from Buford's. Bunny took my order without saying anything extra. That was okay with me.

I said, "The usual."

She said, "And that would be..."

"A burger like always."

"And how would you like it cooked?"

"Oh, knock it off, Bunny, and bring the fucking burger."

"My, my. Testy, aren't we?" She left to put in my order.

I sat while I waited for the burger and went over my notes, trying to figure out what the next step would be.

Perhaps Rodney's search for other witness protection clients would provide a lead. I could only imagine how my visits to them would be received.

"Hi," I'd say. "I understand you're in the witness protection program."

I'd be about as welcome as Charles Manson and his bevy of blade-slinging bitches.

Bunny brought my burger and sat down across from me, interrupting my deep thoughts. She just sat and looked at me. Then she said, "Aren't you even going to talk to me?"

I wanted to, but Willa's and Sammy's advice had taken hold. This was not the time to cave in and set myself up for yet another letdown.

I took a big bite of burger, chewed it up, and swallowed. Then I took a gulp of coffee. Then I wiped my face with my napkin. Then I answered.

"I thought we already understood that you weren't to talk to me." I said.

"We can't go on like this, Stan."

"Why not?"

"We are friends, aren't we?"

"No," I said. "We are not. We are former lovers, one of which dumped the other for the last time. Now go away, and leave me alone."

She sat and fiddled with a napkin, folding it and unfolding it as if the small task gave her a reason to stay.

"I didn't keep the date," she said.

"What date?"

"With Barry."

"Poor Barry, how did he take it?"

"I don't know. I haven't talked to him."

"You stood him up?"

"Yes."

"Maybe Barry and I can form a club. Bunny Rejects Anonymous. BRA. Has a ring to it."

"Oh, stop it."

"We can have monthly meetings here. Can't wait for the T-shirts. When one of us has an overwhelming urge to call you, he calls his BRA sponsor, who rushes over no matter the time of day or night, and the two of them get drunk together."

"Very funny," she said. "You don't have to be mean." She got up and stomped away. According to Willa, she'd be back. I was counting on that.

I finished lunch and counted the money out. Rodney came in.

"Uncle Stanley, I hoped you'd be here. Can you stay while I have lunch?"

"Sure."

Rodney ran up to the counter and gave Bunny his order. He came back and sat across from me.

"No candy bar and Coke?" I said.

"No. The dental hygienist at my dentist's said I needed to take better care of my teeth."

"You go to the dentist?" That was new.

"I do now."

Apparently Rodney was serious about a professional career.

"What are you going to do with all those low-crotch shorts you used to wear?"

"Mom had a yard sale."

"Heaven help the neighbors."

"Okay, Uncle Stanley, I did some of the research you asked for."

I sat forward. Anything he could get would be better than nothing.

"Did we get anything?"

"Did we ever? You aren't going to believe it."

He sat and looked smug. Bunny brought his lunch, a burger just like I had, and plopped it down without speaking.

"Well," I asked Rodney, "how long do I have to wait to hear it?"

"Brace yourself." He took a bite of the burger and talked through his food. "I found only one person in this area in witness protection."

"Who?"

"Grab your jock strap. It's William Sproles."

"Holy shit! That is something."

Rodney was excited and proud about his find. "That's why I couldn't find anything about them before they moved here. I wasn't looking in the right place."

"Was Vitole blackmailing him?"

"I didn't find any record of it."

"Sproles has a crappy job and house and car payments. He couldn't pay Vitole squat."

"I checked OnlinePay. There's no record of Sproles sending any money to Vitole."

"Well, they were neighbors. Maybe he paid in person."

Rodney shook his head. "I got into their financials pretty deep, Uncle Stanley. I found no record of Sproles paying anyone anything out of the ordinary."

If Sproles wasn't paying money to keep Vitole's mouth shut, how was he doing it? I had a hunch. But it wasn't much more that that.

"Well, that's good to know. Good work, Rodney. See what a haircut and a bath can do for a guy?"

"Now can I go on the next interrogation?"

"No. But you get a bonus."

"I do?"

"Yeah. I'll buy your lunch."

"Thanks a lot."

"Who did Sproles testify against before he went underground?"

"He was an accountant. Used to do the books for a syndicate of drug dealers in Baltimore. He rolled on them when the IRS found shaky bookkeeping in his own personal finances."

I put money on the table for Rodney's burger. Rodney gulped down his meal, chug-a-lugged his coffee, and we left.

Bunny watched us go but didn't say anything.

Chapter 26

Rodney, and I returned to the office. The stairs were getting easier. He added the new information about Sproles to the whiteboard. I sat back, and chewed on it a while. All I had was speculation. Nothing concrete.

Given that William Sproles was in witness protection, and that the late Mario Vitole was a retired handler, I wanted to go back and interrogate Sproles, Marsha Sproles, and Stella Vitole. But I didn't have anything to go on.

This would be one of those occasions where I could have used Bill Penrod's skills in the room. I was hoping for a confession. One of them, two of them, or all of them had something to do with Vitole's killing, of that I was certain. But first I needed more evidence, something to back up my suspicions, something they couldn't deny. I called Buford.

"Are Ramon and Sanford available?"

"I can make them available. When do you want to see them?"

"Right away."

"Come on out."

I drove to the Heights. By now Bob knew me on sight and waved me through the gate. Same with Buford's guards at his gate and his door. The guy at the door told me to go into the study.

Buford, Ramon, and Sanford were in the study. Buford had a drink and sat in one of the easy chairs. The other two stood alongside him.

Buford wasn't wearing his bracelet. I didn't ask.

"You need me to leave?" Buford asked.

"No. There's nothing you can't hear. With luck, what we learn here will get you off the hook. Let's all sit down."

The two employees sat on the leather couch, and I sat in the other chair. I got straight to the point.

"Your alibis don't wash. You weren't here shooting pool all day. Now I know you guys take turns chauffeuring the ladies around when they go shopping or wherever. What I need to know is this. From the time of the murder until when Mr. Overbee was formally charged the next day, is there any time that the Rolls was left in a public place unattended?"

They looked at each other as if one could tell the other what to say.

"We usually stay with the car," Ramon said.

"Except when we don't," Sanford said.

Ramon seemed to want to cover his ass. Sanford didn't seem to care.

"That's what I want to know. When and where was the car out of your sight?"

Buford signaled to Ramon to go get him another drink. "What's the point of all this?" Buford asked me.

"You said it yourself," I said. "Somebody planted that gun. It had to be when none of your people was with the car. Unless, of course, one of your people planted the gun. We are assuming that neither of them did." Ramon returned with Buford's drink. I turned to him and Sanford. "So think, guys, where and when?"

Ramon looked at Buford who said, "Don't worry. You won't get in trouble. Tell the man what he needs to know."

Ramon said, "I went to Starbucks when the ladies were shopping."

"When?"

"One o'clock."

"For how long?"

"Most of the afternoon. I read a book and drank coffee. The ladies called me on my cell phone when they were ready to leave. I guess this is my fault. I am sorry."

"Did you do that any other time?"

"That morning too, Señor. I walked around the mall."

I turned to Sanford. "How about you?" I asked.

"No. I usually take a nap."

"Could anyone have gotten into the trunk while you were sleeping?"

He shot me a look that said I had asked a stupid question. Buford laughed. First time I ever saw him laugh.

I went back to the office and called Bill Penrod.

"Bill, I need a favor."

"Name it."

When Bill said that, he was saying only that you should name it. No promises.

"Can you see if there are surveillance cameras anywhere around Belksdales?"

"I'll call you back."

He called back in about five minutes.

"The whole parking lot is covered. The store maintains them."

"Great. What's chances of getting a warrant for the tapes the day Vitole was killed?"

"Based on what?"

"New evidence." I explained about Sproles being in witness protection and my suspicions.

"That's quite the fishing expedition. I doubt we could get a judge to issue a warrant based on that. Particularly since my boss considers this a closed case and doesn't like you. And because of privacy laws that shroud public surveillance videos."

"I figured as much. Thanks."

I hung up the phone, lit my last cigarette ever and looked at Rodney.

"Did you make that appointment with Overbee?"

"Yes."

"Did it have a good outcome?"

"Yes."

"You understand that I don't know anything about that?"

"Yes."

"Good. Go on line, and see if you can find a blank warrant form for evidence in a criminal case."

Tap, click, tap. "Got it, Uncle Stanley."

"Print a copy on Willa's laser."

He did that and brought the form to me. I scribbled what I wanted on the scratch form and gave it to Rodney.

"Fill in a new copy with a typewriter font, print it, and sign the judge's name."

"You're kidding," he said. "Judge Roy Bean?"

"Sure. Why not?"

I got Roscoe out of the safe and clipped it to my belt. With my official-looking counterfeit warrant in hand, I headed out to go shopping.

Belksdales is on the east side of town in an upscale shopping center north of the Interstate. It's one of the bigger stores there and has its own parking lot.

I went inside and went through the store to management's offices. I asked a receptionist for directions to security. She sent me down a flight of stairs into a small glass-enclosed space with a wrap-around console housing video monitors surrounding a chair. An elderly man in the usual ill-fitting uniform sat dozing in the chair. His name tag said Jim.

I tapped him on the shoulder. He came awake and looked me up and down. Here I was, a man with fading bruises on his face, casts on his arm and leg, and a crutch, and I was interrupting his busy day. He looked annoyed until I flashed the gold P.I. shield at him. He came to attention and said, "Yes, sir. How can I help you?"

The gold shield again. Best thirty bucks I ever spent.

"Got a warrant here for copies of your parking lot videos." I held up the warrant and told him the date and times.

"I should probably run this by the general manager," Jim said, "but he went home. Can you wait until tomorrow?"

"No. This is for a murder investigation. You might have read about it, Jim. A fellow got shot down in the street in one of the southern subdivisions. I'm under a lot of pressure to close this case."

"Oh, yeah. Right near his own house. I remember it was on the news. Didn't you guys get the killer?"

"We did, but our case is weak. He might walk on a technicality. He's rich and can afford the best lawyers. All we have is a limited budget and not enough manpower. Hell, man, you're in law enforcement. You know the job."

He seemed pleased that I included him among the finest.

"Seems the criminals have all the rights and the poor victims ain't got none," Jim said. "Have a seat over there, please. It'll take a bit of time."

I sat and waited while Jim typed on his console's keyboard. After a couple of minutes he got up and brought a DVD and handed it to me.

"Always happy to help my brothers on the force," he said. "Don't take the stairs. There's a freight elevator down that hall. I use it. Ain't getting any younger, myself."

I thanked him, went to the elevator, and up and out to my car. I drove back to the office whistling all the way. I hoped the video would prove my theory.

I gave Rodney the DVD and said, "Watch the whole thing. There will be several clips, one for each camera. Look for the Rolls. Pull off any sequences in which there is activity around the Rolls, and make a video of only those scenes. Put the new video on another DVD, and make three copies. Put one in the safe. I'll take the other two."

"You got it, Uncle Stanley."

Why do people always say that before you get anything?

"No I don't," I said. "But I will after you've done what I ask."

"How do I get into the safe?"

"Willa has the combination. I'll look at the DVD tomorrow. I'm whipped, and I'm out of here."

* * *

Dinner at Ray's was quiet. Bunny tried to ignore me while I ate, but whenever I glanced over at her, she was staring at me and quickly looked away.

I went home alone after I ate. I needed a night off. I had a couple books I wanted to read, and I tried that but couldn't get into either one. The case had me preoccupied. I was dead sure that one of those three people had killed Vitole, and I hoped the DVD would prove it. If it didn't show anyone opening the trunk, then the culprit had to be Ramon or Missy. Neither Buford nor Sanford were stupid enough to keep a murder weapon where the cops would find it. And Serena had an airtight alibi.

I went outside and tried walking up and down the sidewalk without my crutch. That was almost a success. I only fell down once.

A man came running up and helped me to my feet.

"You should get a cane," he said.

I thanked him and went back to the apartment to get my crutch. I drove to Walmart and bought a ten-dollar cane. That worked well, and I went home and put the crutch in the hall closet next to its brother.

I mulled everything over for a while thinking about the case. I couldn't stand it any more. I went outside and drove to the office. I hoped I didn't slip with the cane and fall down the stairs.

I made it upstairs, went in the office, and got the DVD from the safe. There was no way to watch it in the office. Normally, we'd use Rodney's laptop, but he'd taken it home with him. Maybe Willa's computer could do it, but I didn't know how.

I went back to the apartment and watched the DVD. Rodney had done a good job of editing. It started with Buford's Rolls pulling up to the curb at about nine in the morning. Serena got out and walked away from the car.

I could've stayed right there watching Serena walk, but I had work to do.

The scene changed to the parking lot where the Rolls pulled into a space. Ramon got out and walked away. The scene faded out and then back in when the car left the parking space. The time stamp showed it to be about eleven o'clock.

The next scene, at about noon, showed the Rolls returning, pulling up to the curb, and letting Missy out. Then the car parked in another space, and Ramon got out and walked away.

So far, the video bore out what Ramon had told me. The surprise came next.

At about one-thirty a panel van pulled up next to the Rolls. I could make out the Arnold Locksmith and Security logo on the side. The driver got out and looked around. The resolution of the video wasn't good enough to clearly show his face, but it was William Sproles, there was no doubt about that. The shape of his head, his hair, and his mannerisms all fit. I wished we could do what they do on CSI and zoom in and sharpen the image, but that's only on television.

Sproles was holding a box. He took the box to the rear of the Rolls and opened the trunk.

Sproles returned to the van, got something else, which could have been a gun. He put it in the trunk of the Rolls and closed the trunk lid. Then he returned to the van, got in, and drove away.

This was what I needed, a video of someone, anyone planting something in Buford's Rolls where the cops had found the gun. It being someone closely related to the crime made it that much better. Of course, none of the details in the low-res video could clearly identify him or verify without a doubt that that's what he was doing. Any moderately competent defense lawyer would have a field day shooting down the evidence, particularly since it was obtained with a bogus warrant, and given the quality of the video. But maybe it would be enough to coerce a confession.

I was satisfied. I went to bed.

Chapter 27

"Bill, I've got good news and bad news."

Why do people always say that when there's seldom enough good news to offset the bad news? This time was different. The good news was great, and the bad news wasn't all that bad.

I was sitting at my desk spinning the DVD on the tip of a pencil. My cell phone was "on speaker" like they say. Rodney sat at his desk and listened.

"What's the good news?" Bill asked.

"I have evidence that clears Buford Overbee."

Bill sighed. "So what's the good news?"

"Seriously, I have a video of someone planting something in the trunk of his car the day of the murder."

"Okay, what's the bad news?"

"Well, given that your case is in the dumpster, I am hoping you'll help me with the interrogation. We need a confession to wrap it up."

"You want to grill the suspect here in the room?"

"That would be best."

"What do I tell the boss?"

"Tell him you're reinforcing the case against Overbee so that a slick lawyer doesn't get him off."

"How about if I come over there and look at your evidence. With all the budget cuts, I can't commit department resources on a hunch, particularly for a closed case."

"My door is always open, Bill. Look on the bright side. Here we can drink. How soon can you be here?"

"Hear that knock on your door?"

About an hour later, Bill was sitting across from me with a drink in his hand. I told him how I got the video and what the Overbee clan had said about their shopping trip. The date/time stamp on the video established the time frame.

I ran the video start to finish on Rodney's laptop. Bill leaned forward, his elbows on the desk, and watched intently.

"Well, Stan, that sure is a nice piece of evidence," he said when the video had played out.

He turned away from the laptop monitor and sat back in the chair across from my desk. "Only problem is it's circumstantial. You can't make out the face, no clear shot of either license plate, and you can't tell what the guy put in the trunk. Not to mention that we shouldn't even be looking at this thing since the warrant was phony."

"But the coincidences are compelling," I said.

"Let's hear it."

"First," I said, "the panel van is from the company Sproles works for. Second, Sproles was out on a bogus service call at that time. I have a copy of the service order. Next, the image matches his description. Finally, how many white Rolls Royces are there in this town? It goes on and on."

Bill wasn't moved by my arguments. It usually took a lot to get him to back off.

"But there's loose ends too," he said.

"Like what?"

"Like this video was made the afternoon after the killing. Only a few hours. How did he know where the Rolls would be parked that quick? From what you told me, Overbee's wife went shopping on a whim. Where did the gun come from? There's no record of it anywhere, and all of Overbee's guns are unregistered."

I wanted him to see the big picture, but he was buried in the details. Our different approaches to solving crimes always worked off one another. But that was when we were on the same side.

"Even so," I said, "all things taken together, it adds up. Sproles killed Vitole and then planted the gun to frame Overbee."

"I guess that's possible. His wife saw Overbee's car at the Vitole house that morning. But why plant it? Why not just toss the piece in the river?"

"I don't know."

"Well, all these unanswered questions, what do you want to do?"

"Let's get him in the room and beat a confession out of him."

"Get me more, Stan. We don't have enough. Maybe Sproles's wife can add something. Maybe Mrs. Vitole."

I filled his glass. He took a sip and listened.

"Maybe we can turn them all on one another. We interview them separately and offer a deal to the first one that spills, and they rat one another out. It's worked before."

We both lit cigarettes, Bill his next, me my last.

"Where would we do that?" he asked.

"At the house. In the room." The house was headquarters. The room would be one of the interrogation rooms. The best place to question a witness. Police territory and a stark, intimidating place. Made you look for the bright light and rubber hose.

"Not on your Aunt Matilda's straw hat. The boss sees you and me dancing around the squad room with witnesses on a closed case, I go down harder than you did. Ain't gonna happen. I like my job."

"Why not show the video to the boss?"

"That's a thought. He's usually pretty fair when it looks like we have the wrong perp. He'll be pissed though. Reopening a closed case always gets attention upstairs."

"Who's prosecuting?"

"ADA Weatherly. New guy."

"Okay. Here's what let's do. Get Weatherly in. Show him the video. Tell him Overbee's lawyer has it, which he will. The defense will be allowed to use it in court because it's exculpatory. Tell them they'll have lots of egg on their face in court and in the press if it comes out that they knew about it and prosecuted anyway."

Bill looked at me with a worried look on his face.

"Stan, what if they find out how you got it?"

"How could they? I didn't leave a copy of the warrant. The rent-a-cop was so happy to be working with the police, that he never asked for it."

That didn't seem to satisfy Bill, who didn't like to speculate.

"But he'll tell them you had one. And that you flashed a badge and impersonated a cop."

"I never said I was a cop. And he didn't see the warrant up close. No big deal. His word against mine."

"We have to tell Weatherly," Bill said. "He has to know everything if he's going to be on our side."

"Okay, I'll tell him the whole enchilada."

"I didn't want it to come to all this, Stan. I'm going to be in a world of hurt. But, I'll survive. I think this video will be enough to get your guy released. They won't be able to use it against the perp, though, because of how you got it."

"Can't you get a real warrant for the videos?"

"Nope. Probable cause comes from your video. Fruit of the poisonous tree. Let's see how this plays out before we figure out what's next."

I gave him a copy of the video.

He pulled his overcoat on. "When do I get to hear the good news?"

Chapter 28

We sat in a conference room in the courthouse. I sat next to Bill Penrod. Across the table from us was ADA Phil Weatherly. Rodney was there in case we had any technical questions, but I had instructed him to observe and speak only when spoken to.

William and Marsha Sproles were in a waiting room while we briefed Weatherly. We showed him the video, and I briefed him on my investigation.

Weatherly excused himself and made a call on his cell phone. When he was done, he said, "That gun was the only piece of physical evidence we had on Overbee, and this video casts a lot of doubt on its credibility. I just talked to the DA. He's releasing Overbee from house arrest as we speak."

Right about then, Bill's cell phone signaled. He pulled it out and looked at it.

"Text from the DA. I am to go pick up the ankle bracelet."

"Overbee will be glad to see you," I said.

"Uncle Stanley, what about—?"

"Shut up, Rodney." Let the cops figure out how Buford got the bracelet off.

Bill sent word for the Sproleses to come in. We introduced them to Weatherly.

"Why are we here?" Sproles asked. "We already told the police every thing we know."

"We need you to look at a video. It might convince you to change your story."

I started the video on Rodney's laptop and turned it around so Mr. and Mrs. Sproles could watch it. Marsha showed no reaction to the video. Sproles himself didn't speak either as the video played. But he turned an ashen shade of gray when he saw the service van pull up next to the Rolls.

When the video showed him getting out of the van, he said, "I think I need a lawyer."

"This is not an official interrogation," Weatherly said. "You haven't been charged or read your rights. Nothing you tell us can be used against you. We're just trying to tie up some loose ends, this visit to Overbee's car being one of them."

Sproles just sat there, saying nothing.

"If you don't want to talk to us, that's okay," Bill said. "Just listen to what we have to say."

Sproles sat there with his lips tightly closed and his arms folded, glaring at me.

"We know you are in witness protection," Bill said.

Sproles reacted visibly.

Bill continued. "We know Vitole used to be a handler. We know that he had been blackmailing witness protection clients. We know that he had been having an affair with your wife."

Bill slid copies across the table of the pictures I had taken of Vitole and Marsha. Sproles looked at the pictures, put his face in his hands, and rocked from side to side. Marsha Sproles still didn't react.

"And we know from this video that you planted the murder weapon in Overbee's car."

"I do need a lawyer," Sproles said.

"Yes, you do," Weatherly said. "So don't talk if you don't want to. But listen."

Bill continued.

"This can go several ways. If the feds see this video, or if we charge you with this murder, tampering with evidence, or anything else, you're out of witness protection and back in prison."

"And dead," Sproles added. "Marsha too. They'll figure she knows what I know."

"Who's they?" Weatherly asked.

"Drug dealers in Baltimore," Sproles said. "The guys I am testifying against."

"So you see what's at stake here," Bill said. "If you want any kind of deal, you better talk to us now. You can get a lawyer if you want, but as soon as that happens, all deals are off the table and you get charged with, at the very least, accessory after the fact. At the worst, first degree murder. A date with the needle."

Marsha Sproles spoke up for the first time. "That video. You can't tell that it's William. The details are blurred."

"That's because we're watching the raw version," I said. "The enhanced version is still being processed. It will show not only your husband's face but the license plate numbers too."

"Uh, Uncle Stanley—," Rodney said.

"Not now, Rodney."

"But—," he said.

"Clam up and observe," I said. He did. I wanted them to believe that the lab could do what they'd seen done on CSI, NCIS, and other cop shows countless times. It was all bullshit, but they didn't know that.

"What kind of deal would you offer?" Sproles asked.

"You confess, and we prosecute you under your new name. The Baltimore crowd never finds out it's you. We take the death penalty off the table. We intervene with the feds on your behalf to maintain your protection. You do twenty-five to life."

Marsha started crying. "Prison? For twenty-five years? No, I won't let that happen."

"Marsha, don't," Sproles said.

"No, William, I have to." She reached over, put her hand on her husband's arm, and looked at Bill. "I shot Mario Vitole," she said. "William didn't have anything to do with it."

"Mirandize both of them," Weatherly said. "Now."

Bill read William and Marsha their rights. Then he said, "You realize this makes William an accessory. We'll have to deal with that."

"I understand," she said. "But it's better than murder."

"Do you want to waive your right to legal counsel?" he asked.

"Yes, I waive them."

"How about you, Mr. Sproles?"

"Yes," Sproles said.

People are dumb about giving up their rights. If I was a suspect, I wouldn't say squat to the cops without a lawyer. Bill and I had used this kind of ignorance to get confessions and close cases many times.

Bill turned on the voice recorder on his cell phone and put it in the middle of the conference table. He said the date and time, his name, the names of the others in the room, and that the Sproleses had been read and had waived their rights. Then he said, "Proceed with your statement, Mrs. Sproles. Start with your name and address and then tell us everything that happened."

She wiped her eyes, blew her nose, and started in. "My name is Marsha Sproles. I live at 512 Cherokee Avenue, Delbert Falls, Maryland. About three months ago, Mario Vitole visited me during the day. He said he knew my husband and I were in witness protection. He said if I'd have sex with him during the day, William and Stella didn't need to know, and he wouldn't tell the people in Baltimore where we were."

This was what I had suspected. But up until now, it had been only a hunch. Now, I would have shot the asshole myself.

"I had no choice but to succumb," she said. "I told him every time that I didn't want to do it, but he made me do it."

"How did you happen to shoot him?" Bill asked.

"Every time he wanted to see me, usually two or three times a week in the morning, he'd call to say he was coming up. Sometimes I'd have company in, maybe another housewife in the neighborhood, but I could only use that excuse sometimes. Finally, I had enough. When he called that morning, I went out into the street as if to greet him. When he was close enough, I shot him."

"Where did you get the gun?" Bill asked.

"It was his. He used to carry it in his pocket. He had put it on my nightstand one time when he undressed. I guess he forgot it. I hid it in a drawer, and he never asked about it."

Bill turned off the voice recorder.

"Probably his drop gun when he was on the job," Bill said.

"What's a drop gun," she asked.

Bill nodded to me, and I explained. "Sometimes cops carry untraceable guns for when they shoot an unarmed person. They drop the gun on the perp so it looks like he was carrying. The practice makes righteous shoots out of on-duty mistakes."

She shook her head and looked at the floor. Bill turned the recorder on again.

"How did your husband get involved?" Bill asked.

"I called him and told him what happened and why. He came home, took the gun, told me to call the police and report the body. Then he left."

Bill spoke into the recorder. "This next question is addressed to Mr. William Sproles. Mr. Sproles, please state your name and address."

"William Sproles, 512 Cherokee Avenue, Delbert Falls, Maryland."

"Tell us what you did with the gun after your wife gave it to you."

"I went back to work and got the master key set for Rolls Royces. Then I took the gun to Mr. Overbee's car, opened the trunk, and put the gun in the trunk."

"How did you know to put it in Overbee's car specifically?"

"Marsha had told me a white Rolls had been parked there earlier that morning."

"How did you know where the Rolls would be?"

"A coincidence. When I was coming home, I drove past Belksdales and saw it pull into the parking lot ahead of me. You tend to notice a Rolls."

"And did you know that Mr. Overbee owned a white Rolls?"

"No. I don't know him, never met him, never heard his name until you guys arrested him."

"Why didn't you just toss the gun in the river?"

"I might have been seen on the bridge in the van. This way, it would just look like a service call for somebody who locked their keys in the car. And that if you guys found it, it might divert suspicion away from Marsha."

He hadn't been thinking straight. Anything happening around a Rolls Royce would be noticed. But I gave him credit for a creative solution to his problem.

Bill turned the recorder off. "Well, what do you think, Mr. Weatherly?" he asked

"The only case you stand a chance of making is a charge of tampering with evidence. And no jury would convict on that after hearing this story."

"What about Mrs. Sproles?" Bill said. "She confessed to the murder."

"Self-defense. You heard her. The guy was raping her on a regular basis. She couldn't call you guys about the rape, and she couldn't tell you about the shooting. Their witness protection cover would be blown. I think a judge would toss it out. Mr. and Mrs. Sproles, you are free to go."

William and Marsha Sproles got up from the table and left without saying anything. I couldn't blame them.

"Well, at least I still have a closed case," Bill said. "That ought to keep the bosses happy."

"If I was to bring charges against anyone," Weatherly said, "It would be against Bentworth here for impersonating a police officer and counterfeiting a court document."

Bill started laughing. I didn't.

"But I won't," Weatherly said. "Call it gratitude for acting in the name of justice. Or, more accurately call it a case I probably couldn't even get an indictment on."

Chapter 29

Back at the office, Rodney made the final entries on the whiteboard. He photographed it for the files and wiped it clean. The Overbee case was closed.

His cell phone rang, and he answered it.

"It's Mom," he said. "She's crying."

"Give me the phone...Mandy, what's wrong?"

"Jeremy is back, Stanley," she said. "He called me here at the office. He's coming to see me tonight."

"Here we go again," I said. "Don't worry. Rodney and I will be there like before. How come you didn't call me?"

"I did. You didn't answer."

I pulled out my phone. Dead battery. I had forgotten to charge it again.

"What time do you get home?"

"About five-thirty."

"We'll meet you there."

I hung up and turned to Rodney. "Go home, and wait inside. That Captain Pugh is back."

"I thought he got blown up."

"Apparently not. He's coming there sometime tonight. Lock the doors and windows, and wait for your mother. I'll be there after a while."

I dug around in my jacket pockets until I found the card for the CID guy, Stewart. I tried to call, but my phone was dead. The AC adaptor was home in my apartment, and Willa was on the land line, so I went down to my car where I had an adaptor. It didn't work. Bad connection or a malfunctioning cigarette lighter receptacle or something. I walked from the car back to the office and went up. I'd wait for the phone. Besides, I had forgotten Roscoe and didn't want to go on this adventure without heat.

Willa was off the phone. "What got into Rodney?" she asked.

"What do you mean?"

"After you left, he came tearing in here, went in your office, came tearing out, and was gone in a flash."

I went in my office. The safe was open and Roscoe was gone. Somehow, Rodney had gotten into the safe and was on his way to his house with Roscoe. I looked at Mickey. Quarter to five. I had time to make my call, get there ahead of Amanda, and take Roscoe away from Rodney before he shot himself in the foot. I used the office land line to call Stewart.

"USACIDC. Stewart here."

"This is Stanley Bentworth. Are you still looking for the missing Captain Jeremy Pugh?"

"Yes, assuming he's alive."

"He is. He's coming to my sister's house tonight, probably some time after five thirty."

"Give me the address. We'll be there."

I read off Amanda's address and hung up.

Then I called Buford.

"Is the bracelet off?"

"Has been for a while."

"Somebody should be there to get it soon. Your charges have been dropped."

"I don't know how to thank you," Buford said. He sounded like he was about to cry. I'd have paid money to see that.

"I do need help," I told Buford. "That Army captain is back."

"Help is on the way," Buford said.

I gave him Amanda's address and hung up.

I went into the outer office. Willa was about to leave.

"You have a wall adaptor to charge a phone."

"Right here."

I hooked it up and left the cell phone there.

"How did Rodney get into the safe?"

"Back when he made you that DVD. He said you said I should give him the combination."

"Sneaky little shit. That's not what I told him."

"Sorry. I wondered at the time."

"It's okay. Call Bill Penrod, and tell him there's trouble at Amanda's house. Captain Pugh is back. I've got CID on the way. I don't know what's going to happen, but Rodney took my gun and is probably there by now. Tell Bill not to shoot Rodney."

I figured between Rodney, CID, the cops, and whatever Buford sent, I might just have an edge.

Chapter 30

I left the office and went to my car as fast as the cane and cast would allow. Ten minutes later I was at Amanda's house. Rodney's truck was parked in front. There was no sign of him or anyone else on the premises.

I went to the door and tried to open it. It was locked. I listened but couldn't hear anything. I walked around the house looking in windows. Most of them were covered with curtains. You'd think I'd have remembered that having lived in the house for several miserable days, but I don't pay attention to curtains.

I did remember that the kitchen window over the sink had no window dressing. I had often looked out into the back yard when I washed dishes for Amanda. I got up on tiptoe, not easy with a leg in a cast, and looked in. Rodney sat on the floor next to the refrigerator tied with a pair of pantyhose and gagged. I had to let myself down before I fell down.

I went up again to look in. Rodney began to twist around, trying to say something. He was agitated and couldn't make more than a muffled yell through the gag, which I recognized as one of my old socks. I hoped it was clean.

I heard the front door open and close followed by a scream, loud at first then muffled. It was Amanda. I'd heard that same scream one day when a mouse ran across the kitchen floor.

I stretched up and looked in the window again. Nothing happened for a while. Then Jeremy Pugh came into the kitchen dragging Amanda tied and gagged like Rodney. Her face was distorted with fear, and she tried to cry out, but the gag, one of her own stockings, kept her from yelling.

Jeremy looked up and saw me. His hand came up, and he pointed Roscoe directly at me. I dropped to the ground and Roscoe spoke for the first time since I'd gotten him. The bullet drilled a small round hole in the window pane and went over me out into the back. I hoped it didn't hit another house.

He knew I was here now, but he didn't know whether I was armed. Which is probably all that kept him from coming to the back door and finishing me off.

I went around to the front of the house. I wanted to call him and do some hostage negotiation, but my cell phone was back at the office getting charged. I got close to the front of the house near a window and yelled, "Jeremy!"

No response. I yelled again. Then the window opened, and an awesome sight presented itself. Dad's old shotgun barrel came sticking out the window. I didn't want to call out again. I didn't want him to figure out where I was from the direction of my voice. I kept quiet.

"Bentworth? You still out there? Speak up. I won't shoot."

Could I trust him? What else could I do? I spoke quietly. "I'm here Jeremy. What do you want?"

"I want Amanda. You people keep getting in the way. Her kid comes in here waving a pistol and then you. All I want is to talk to her."

"So you tie her up and toss her in the kitchen?"

"She started screaming. I just wanted to talk."

"What are you going to do?"

"I don't know."

"Why don't you come out, and you and I can talk?"

"I come out, I come out shooting. You had my two best friends killed."

Probably his only friends.

"That wasn't me, Jeremy. I had a beef with those two guys after the beat-down, but I don't shoot people. Besides, the cops checked my piece. It wasn't me."

"Okay, I'll hold off until I'm sure. But if you're lying..."

"Okay, Jeremy. Just don't hurt anyone. Don't let it get out of control. You haven't done anything really bad yet. Let's keep it that way while we figure out where this is going."

A black SUV pulled up across the street. Sanford got out and stood there in his ill-fitting black suit and a black trench coat. He watched me to see what would happen.

"Who's that guy over there?" Jeremy said.

"That's someone who can help you get out of here unharmed. I'll go talk to him. Don't shoot."

I went across the street to where Sanford stood.

"Need help? The boss says we owe you."

"I figured we were even after those two army guys and the wise guy."

"Don't know what you're talking about. You want help or not?"

"I could use some." I explained what was happening.

"I can take him. Clear shot."

"There's a direct line from here into the kitchen. You might hit one of the hostages."

"Okay. What can I do?"

"How about you go in the back door into the kitchen. Get my sister and nephew out while I'm talking to Pugh. Shoot him if you have to, but I have the cops and the Army on the way. They can take him out. Save you the trouble of explaining anything. And the paperwork."

"And them checking my piece." He patted the left side of his chest.

"You got bodies on that piece?"

"Could be."

That figured.

"Okay. Wait until I get back to the window. Then drive around the block, and come in from the rear so he can't see you coming. You'll need a knife to cut them loose. They're tied with stockings. Butcher knives are on the countertop."

Sanford pulled a long switchblade from his pocket and held it up.

"That'll do," I said.

I walked back towards the house, hoping Jeremy would keep his promise not to shoot me. The shotgun barrel was still sticking out the window. I made it to the wall.

"Where's that guy going?" Jeremy asked.

"Putting his car out of sight so no one can see him help you escape."

"Why would he do that."

"I asked him to. To save Amanda and Rodney."

"I'm not going to hurt them."

"Good." I had to keep him talking. "What happened with your boat?"

"I got it blown up. They were going to repossess it, and I needed to drop out of sight. I thought maybe my wife and kids could use the insurance if they thought I was dead."

"Why did you need to drop out of sight?"

"The brass got it in their heads that I was stalking Amanda. Sent me to an Army shrink. He was talking about confinement."

"You didn't think that might help you?"

"No, goddammit. There's nothing wrong with me."

Add denial to this fruitcake's disorders.

"Who did the explosive device?"

"An army demolition guy I served with in Iraq. We set it off with a cell phone. You should've seen it go."

This was good. He was starting to talk to me like we were old friends. Probably the manic side of his disorder kicking in.

"How about letting Amanda and Rodney go?"

"Can't. They're my insurance."

That didn't make sense. How did he think holding two civilians hostage would keep him out of the loony bin?

"Where's that guy at?" he asked.

"He's over there." I pointed to the side of the house out of Jeremy's sight. "I can see him." I couldn't, but I didn't want Jeremy to start worrying about where Sanford was. I had to keep him diverted.

"Where did you meet your two friends? The ones that got shot?"

"Years ago. At the Moose lodge. We were like brothers. They made a good team."

"I'll say, and I have the bandages to show for it."

"Sorry about that."

"Yeah, me too. I think you and I could've been friends under different circumstances."

Fat chance.

"Shit!" Jeremy said.

"What?" I looked behind me. Two Army vehicles were pulling up across the street where Sanford had been parked. Stewart and his two associates got out of one. Four MPs in full SWAT gear got out of the other.

"Wait, Jeremy," I said. "I'll go talk to them. You're safe as long as you're holed up in there and have Amanda and Rodney."

I hobbled over to the Army cars where Stewart and his entourage were waiting, crouched behind their cars, guns aimed at the house.

"How did you know it was this much trouble," I asked. "When I called, I didn't know he was here yet."

"We know the Captain," Stewart said.

"He's in the house at the window," I told Stewart. "He has an old shotgun and my pistol. He has hostages, my sister and her son."

"A child?"

"No. Teenager. They're both tied up in the kitchen at the rear of the house. I have a man sneaking in the back way to get them out while we keep Pugh occupied."

"Isn't your man likely to get hurt going in there like that?"

"He can take care of himself. Pugh has been getting chummy, so maybe we can talk him out. Do you know him?"

"Yes. He's been on our radar for a while. Had to pull him out of Afghanistan. Post traumatic stress disorder. He ought to be in a hospital."

"I need to go back and keep him talking."

"Well don't trust him to stay friendly. He has a short fuse. One minute he's your pal, the next minute he's in your face yelling and screaming."

"So I've seen. My guy will sneak the hostages out and, your guys can deal with the short fuse."

"Okay, we can give it a try if you think your man can handle it."

"He can. Pugh told me that he had his boat blown up to fake his death so you guys wouldn't send him to the funny farm."

"Figures. My guys can take him out. He's in clear view in the window. Fool."

"Absolutely not. Let's get the hostages out first."

Stewart looked at me as if to ask where I got the authority to run a hostage situation. Before he could raise the question, an unmarked police car pulled up. Bill Penrod got out and came over to where we were crouched behind the Army cars.

"What's going on here, Stan? Willa called."

I explained the situation to him.

"I better get our SWAT team over here," he said.

Everybody wanted to shoot this guy. Must have been a slow SWAT day.

"Look around, Sergeant," Stewart said. "We have ours in place and ready."

"So you do," Bill said. "But these are civilian hostages on civilian premises. The police department has jurisdiction."

"Hey, guys," I said. "It's kind of busy here. Let's not get into a turf war."

A black SUV turned the corner and came towards us. It pulled up behind Bill's car and stopped. Sanford held a skinny arm out the window and gave me a thumbs up. I went to the SUV and looked in. Amanda and Rodney were in the back seat looking frightened and tussled but none the worse for wear. I grinned at them and went back to Bill and the Army.

"He's all yours, guys. The hostages are out."

"Is there a phone in there?" Stewart asked.

"Yes, on a table next to the window." I said and gave him the number. He called. We could hear the phone ringing through the open window. After about seven rings, it stopped.

Stewart said, "Captain Pugh. This is Special Agent Stewart, USACIDC. We got the hostages out. You're all alone. You want to come out, or would you rather die today?"

"Man," I said to Bill, "That's a hell of a way to negotiate."

He shrugged and said, "I wouldn't do it that way. I guess they have their methods."

Stewart turned to me. "He wants to talk to you." I took the phone.

"What's up, Jeremy?"

"Bentworth, this is going to come to a bad end, I can tell. Those guys want to shoot me."

"It doesn't have to happen. What can I do?"

"Come back up here so we can talk without them listening in."

"You won't shoot me, will you?"

"No. I give my word."

Do you take the word of the guy who tried to have you killed then took your sister and nephew hostage? I wasn't sure.

About five police cars, an ambulance, and a fire truck turned onto our street, lights flashing, sirens quiet.

"I called them," Bill said.

The cops stopped, piled out of their vehicles, and crouched behind them. More guns came out and were pointed at the house.

"The militia is here Jeremy," I said. "They've got guns trained on you. They're ready to take you down. Get back away from the window. I'll call you again and let you know what's happening."

I hung up.

"Why'd you tell him that?" Bill said. "Now we might have to put men at risk."

"Wait," I said. "There's an easier way."

I went over to Sanford's SUV.

"You think you can get him out of there without killing him?" I asked Sanford.

"Piece of cake," he said.

I went over to Bill and Stewart.

"I don't want my sister's house all shot up," I said. "And let's not be so quick to shoot this guy. He's sick. My colleague and I can get him out. Hold your fire, and let us try."

"Okay," Bill said, looking at his watch. "But only because it's you. You got ten minutes. Then we go in. You agree, Agent Stewart?"

"Yes."

I went over to Sanford's SUV and said, "Let's go."

He got out of the SUV keeping his back to all the cops and soldiers. We walked down the sidewalk away from them and the row of official vehicles, more or less out of sight of the house.

"Can you walk any faster?" Sanford asked.

"Not much," I said.

"Okay. I'm going ahead. Go down half a block, turn up the side street, and come to the back door. It'll be open. You can just walk in."

"What if you don't have him?"

He looked at me like he couldn't believe his ears.

"Sorry," I said. "Proceed."

He went off at a medium trot, his black trench coat flapping in the breeze. I followed at a slow cane-assisted stroll. It took a while, and I was worried about Bill's ten minute deadline.

When I got to the back door, it was open. I went in, looked from side to side, scanned the kitchen, and peered into the dining room. Nothing in sight, no sounds.

I felt naked entering an unsecured crime scene without Roscoe. Old habits die hard. I moved cautiously across the kitchen. My cast and cane made thump, thump sounds. I couldn't help it.

Sanford called out, "Come on in, Bentworth. I got him."

I went in and found Sanford holding his gun on Jeremy, who was on his knees, his hands cuffed behind his back. The shotgun was on the floor, and Roscoe was on the coffee table. I went over, picked it up, and stuck it in my belt.

"Any trouble taking him?"

He gave me that look again.

"Where'd you get the cuffs," I asked.

"Keep them. I have others. You can take him outside. I'm out of here."

He want back through the kitchen and out the back door. I opened the front door and yelled, "Hold your fire, we're coming out."

I leaned over Jeremy, took hold of his cuffs with my good hand, and pulled him up to his feet. He helped, so it wasn't that difficult. I pushed him ahead of me and stepped out onto the stoop. In no time at all, two policemen had him on the ground, were putting their own cuffs on him, and reading him his rights. Just like on television. Except the cops weren't all that handsome.

They tossed Sanford's cuffs to me. A souvenir. Never had my own cuffs since I left the force. I'd need a key. No problem. Once size fits all. The cuffs could keep Roscoe company in the safe.

For the first time in hours I breathed easily. My injuries were aching from the walk and the stress. I needed to sit down.

Jeremy looked up at me and said, "I thought I could trust you."

"I saved your life, Jeremy. If these cops didn't get you, that shotgun would've blown up in your face. I just hope you get the help you need."

Don't ask why I gave a shit about his welfare, given all the grief he'd handed down. Just my nature, I guess.

Sanford's SUV backed away from the curb and into a driveway. Amanda and Rodney got out. The SUV pulled onto the road, turned away from us, and drove away.

Bill walked up. "Your friend is leaving. I never got a look at him. Who was it?"

"An associate," I said. If Sanford didn't want to talk to cops, I wasn't going to intervene.

"Did you cut Overbee loose?" I asked.

"Not exactly. He cut himself loose. I went with the tech guy to get the bracelet after our meeting this morning. When we got to his house, there were reporters all over the place. I don't know how they got past the guard."

"Old Bob? Probably time for his nap."

"The ankle bracelet was already off Overbee and on the leg of a statue in the foyer. He didn't tell me how it got there, and I didn't ask."

Good for Rodney. I could forgive him for pinching Roscoe as long as he never did it again. I walked over to him. "Where's my holster?"

"In my truck."

"Go get it."

He went to his truck and returned with the holster. I put the pistol in it and clipped it to my belt.

"What made you try a stunt like that?"

"The guy's a nut, Uncle Stanley. He was coming after my Mom. You're all crippled up. Somebody had to do something."

"So what did you learn from all this?"

"Learn?"

"Yes, learn. What did you learn?"

"Not to take your gun?"

"No. You learned that having a gun doesn't make you the baddest badass on the block. You walked right into it. He took the gun away from you, and you're lucky he didn't shoot you with it."

"He was already in the house when I got there, but I didn't know that. When I went in, he was standing there pointing Grandpa's shotgun at me. He tied me up, and when Mom got home he tied her up."

"Yeah. I heard all that."

"What'll happen to him?"

"The cops and the Army will have to fight that out. I don't care as long as they put him away somewhere for a long time."

Amanda said, "I'm proud of both of you."

She rubbed Rodney's hair, and he squirmed to get out from under her caresses.

"That man who got us out of there," she said, "we met him in the hospital. Who is he?"

"A very good friend named Sanford. Wants to maintain some distance. But we all owe him big time."

Rodney said, "I feel a 'hiyo, Silver' coming on."

"I should cook dinner for him," Amanda said.

"I'll pass the invitation on. He'll say thanks and decline. But you owe him your lives. Chances are if the cavalry had come storming in, Pugh would have killed both of you before they got him."

Neighbors started to come out of their houses and line the sidewalk. They watched the vehicles pull out. Amanda and Rodney went into the house. The neighbors talked among themselves, speculating about what had taken place.

A Channel 6 news van pulled up. Late to the party. A cameraman and a pretty woman holding a microphone got out.

"What happened here?" the woman asked, her microphone stuck in my face and the camera pointed at me and grinding away.

"Beats the shit out of me," I said and walked away towards my car. The news team went to interview neighbors. I hoped they'd leave Amanda alone. If not, Rodney could tell them how he had saved his mother from a horde of madmen, home invaders, stalkers, and rapists.

I got in my car and headed to the office. On the way I stopped at the liquor store to get another jug. This time I got the good stuff, went to the office, climbed the stairs, got my cell phone from Willa's desk, and sat alone at my desk. I sipped bourbon and thought about the day. Two cases closed on one shift. It doesn't get any better than that.

I looked at my cell phone. Buford had called. I punched the re-dial button. He answered right away.

"Sanford called," Buford said. "He says you got your Army problem cleared up," he said.

"Yes, I did with his help. I can't thank you guys enough."

"You earned it. I've got to clear out of here. The mob knows where I live and who I am now. Hell, the whole fucking world knows who I am and what I look like. Reporters and cameras all over the place."

"Maybe Sanford can shoo them off."

"Yeah. Well, anyway, I'm out of here. Want to buy a mansion? Real estate's way down."

"Where will you go?"

"Offshore. I can run my business just as easily from some is-land. I never did get face-to-face with most of my clients anyway. And Serena can get that year-round tan she's always wanted."

"And you can be closer to your money."

"Right." He laughed for the second time since we'd met. "Thanks for everything, Stan. If I ever need somebody found, I'll call. Do I owe you any money?"

"No. We're good. Keep in touch."

There goes my perpetual retainer, I thought. I knew it was too good to be true.

I didn't want to get drunk tonight, so I paced myself and used the time to update the files on the Overbee case. There were no files on the Jeremy Pugh case, it being a personal matter, so I wrote entries in my journal to capture for posterity all the rele-vant times and events. Maybe I'll write a book some day.

Chapter 31

I got home at about nine o'clock. I was hungry. A pizza slice or something edible might be in the freezer. I had a surprise waiting.

Bunny sat on the stoop in front of my door, a big grocery bag on the sidewalk next to her. She gave me that doe-eyed look. I knew she was playing me, and it was working.

"Can I come in?"

"What for?" I wasn't about to give in right away. I intended to be strong.

"I brought groceries. I can fix you some supper."

Strong, my ass. I am one weak son-of-a-bitch. The combination of the woman I want and a home-cooked meal was too much. My resolve collapsed.

"Come on in," I said with a heavy sigh.

We went into my apartment, and I tossed the cane in a corner and collapsed on the couch.

"I've had a day," I said.

"You can tell me about it after I get this going."

She took a bottle of wine out of the grocery bag and opened it. Wine? I don't drink wine. But my only jug of bourbon was at the office. So, I lit a cigarette and sipped the wine.

She unloaded the rest of the groceries. "I thought you quit smoking."

"Not in months with an 'R'."

She got supper going on the stove and came over, pushed me onto my side against the back of the sofa, stretched out beside me, and began unbuttoning my shirt. She took the burned-down cigarette out of my mouth and stamped it out in the ashtray. The kiss she followed up with was to die for.

"The Spoiler," I said.

"What?"

I said under my breath, "Two stones that pass in the night."

"What?"

"Nothing, Bunny. Just thinking out loud."

"Now you can tell me about your day," she said, cuddling up and kissing my chest.

"Oh, nothing special," I said. "Just your typical boring, routine day in the life of a private investigator."

I lit my last cigarette ever and settled in.

Also by Al Stevens

The Shadow on the Grassy Knoll
A Dead Ringer (Stanley Bentworth #2)
Confessions of a Cat Burglar
Clueless (Stanley Bentworth #3)
Off the Wall Stories
Golden Eagle's Final Flight (with Ron Skipper)
Ventriloquism: Art, Craft, Profession
Politically Incorrect Scripts for Comedy Ventriloquists
Welcome to Programming
Teach Yourself C++ 7th Edition
...and many other computer programming and usage books.

http://www.alstevens.com

About the Author

Al Stevens is a retired author of computer programming books. For fifteen years he was a senior contributing editor and columnist for Dr. Dobb's Journal, a leading magazine for computer programmers.

Al lives with his wife Judy and a menagerie of cats on Florida's Space Coast where he writes by day and plays piano, string bass, and saxophone by night.